THE TWO F

CW00860107

Lan and Jenny strolled over to take a closer look. It was a handsome bike, Lan had to admit, with its sleek black fairing lettered in gold: Kawasaki Twin-Cam 16-Valve. Then he walked around the back of the motorcycle and froze. The racy script on the tailpipe leaped out at him. NINJA. *Ninja?* Was there a connection, or was this just a coincidence?

Lan's brain raced to add up what he knew about Ninja and Adam: older brothers, younger brothers, money problems. It *could* be a coincidence, he concluded; but his gut told him it wasn't.

The Hotline series

The characters and situations in this book are entirely imaginary and bear no relation to any real person or actual happenings.

HOTLINE
BOOK 4

The Two Faces of Adam

Carolyn Meyer

Hodder & Stoughton
LONDON SYDNEY AUCKLAND

Copyright 1990 by Carolyn Meyer and General Licensing Company, Inc.

Cover art copyright © 1990 by General Licensing Company, Inc.

First published in the U.S.A. by Bantam Books in 1990

First published in Great Britain by Hodder and Stoughton Ltd in 1992

The right of Carolyn Meyer to be identified as the author of this work has been asserted by her in accordance with the Copyright, Designs and Patents Act 1988.

This book is sold subject to the condition that it shall not, by way of trade or otherwise, be lent, re-sold, hired out or otherwise circulated without the publisher's prior consent in any form of binding or cover other than that in which it is published and without a similar condition including this condition being imposed on the subsequent purchaser.

No part of this publication may be reproduced or transmitted in any form or by any means, electronic or mechanical, including photocopying, recording or any information storage or retrieval system, without either the prior permission in writing from the publisher or a licence, permitting restricted copying. In the United Kingdom such licences are issued by the Copyright Licensing Agency, 90 Tottenham Court Road, London WC1P 9HE.

British Library C.I.P.

A catalogue record for this book is available from the British Library

ISBN 0-340-58005-4

Printed and bound in Great Britain for Hodder and Stoughton Children's Books, a division of Hodder and Stoughton Ltd., Mill Road, Dunton Green, Sevenoaks, Kent TN13 2YA (Editorial Office: 47 Bedford Square, London WC1B 3DP) by Clays Ltd, St Ives plc.

PART I

Overload

Wednesday, January 3

I *just don't understand*, Lan Nguyen thought. *How could such things happen? Two students dead.*

It was the first day back after Christmas break, and the news had stunned the school. Sometime last night, in separate incidents, two Roosevelt High School students had died.

Lan looked around the room at his classmates and fellow hotline members and wondered how many of them were remembering Lissa Mainzer. Another senseless death. Her suicide last September had been the catalyst for the hotline, a place kids could call and talk about whatever was on their minds to someone who would really listen.

Now it looked as though it was the hotliners who needed to talk. They were gathered in Temporary 3-A with their two advisors for their first regular meeting since before the holiday, pooling the skimpy information gleaned from rumors to try to figure out what had happened. All they knew for sure was that Joseph Di-Angelis and Karen Garcia wouldn't be coming back. Ever.

"How did it happen?" Kurt Lundquist asked Mr. Montgomery. "Do you know anything about it?"

"All I've heard," the bearded advisor replied, "is that Joseph died of an apparent drug overdose, and Karen was killed instantly when her car was struck by a drunk driver."

"Mr. Duckworth is coming by later," added Ms. Hawkins, their other advisor. "Maybe he can tell us something more."

Lan Nguyen raked his fingers through his thick, dark hair and listened tensely to the conversations, his stomach clenching. How could such things happen? He didn't know either of the students personally, but he was still shocked. The loss sickened him.

"I had classes with both of them," Michelle Piper whispered, her voice breaking. "I can't believe it— yesterday they were alive, and today they're dead. I keep asking myself *why*?"

In an instant Angie Montoya was kneeling beside Michelle, murmuring comforting words, her arm around Michelle's shoulders. Lan noticed how pale and gaunt Michelle appeared; her long auburn hair hung limp around her thin shoulders, and her skin had an unhealthy pallor. Had she been ill? Lan wondered.

"Drugs and alcohol, that's why," Jenny Haviland answered Michelle grimly, tugging on a strand of her straight brown hair. "That's what it's all about, and it makes me absolutely furious! The drug problem especially seems to be getting worse all the time in Eldorado. I can't help wondering how many more kids are going to die before somebody figures out what to do about it."

"Well, if people could figure out that they shouldn't do drugs in the first place, there wouldn't be a prob-

4

lem," Jason Aragon offered. "It's the same thing with drinking and driving. Some people never learn."

"It's hard to believe that people still do things they know are bad for them. But they do. Has anybody noticed the number of drug-related calls we've been getting?" Nikki Vavra asked. "I was just looking over the log book, and it seems like a lot of the calls right before the holidays had something to do with drugs."

Lan propped his elbows on his knees and stared at the floor. "I took one of those calls," he said quietly. "A girl who wanted me to call her Star said she was worried about her parents. They smoke marijuana—a lot, she said—and they grow it at their cabin in the mountains. She wanted to know what to do."

The hotliners focused their attention on Lan. "What did you say?" several of them asked at once. They seemed almost relieved to have something definite to discuss.

Lan disliked being in the spotlight, but talking about calls was part of the job, and he tried to reconstruct the conversation accurately. Maybe it would help all of them to get their minds away from two tragedies that couldn't be explained.

"I said I know smoking pot is illegal," he told them, "and growing it is illegal, too. And that her parents could end up in a lot of trouble."

"How did she respond to that, Lan?" Rob Saylor asked. "Because this is very serious stuff. We're talking felony here."

"She said she already knew that and she wanted concrete advice: what should she *do*, exactly? I suggested she could try talking to her parents, tell them she's worried about them and how what they do affects *her*," Lan said. "She said she's been trying, but they won't talk about it. She said she even threatened to turn them in if they didn't quit."

"Turn in her own parents!" Jenny exploded. "That doesn't exactly sound like problem-solving to me."

"It would certainly create a lot of guilt and anxiety," Steven Feldman mused. As a psychiatrist in training, Steven often seemed to think it his duty to issue pompous statements and amateur analyses to his fellow hotliners. Lan saw Ilana flash her brother a "give me a break" look, but the other hotliners nodded in agreement, too caught up in the problem to give Steven a hard time.

"She said she could never really do it," Lan told them, "but she feels really frustrated. She worries about her parents and nothing she says makes any difference. They just keep doing it."

"I'm glad I didn't get that call," Angie Montoya confessed, staying close to Michelle, who kept dabbing at her eyes. "I wouldn't have known what to say. It must be horrible to have parents that do drugs. Because I don't know what you can do to get them to stop. And the idea of turning them in . . ." Angie shuddered.

"It was a hard call," Lan admitted. "That's why I'm glad we always have a partner," he said, looking gratefully at Jack Mertz. While the hotliner on duty sat in the small inner office with the phone, the partner either stayed in there or hung out here in the room they used for meetings, within earshot, ready to help. That way you didn't feel completely on your own if a really difficult call came in, like Star's. He remembered how relieved he had felt that Jack was sitting only a few feet away.

"The strange thing is," Lan continued, "Star says that in every other way her parents are actually pretty great. They all get along fine, and she says they really listen to her."

"Except about this one subject."

"Right."

"So I've been wondering about her ever since. I just don't see how people can get involved in drugs," Lan said. "It doesn't make any sense to me, to mess up your life like that. And not only your own life, but other people's, too. Look what Star's parents are doing to their own daughter!"

"Maybe she'll call back," Jason Aragon suggested. "I hope so."

"Star is going to need a lot of support, no matter how she decides to handle the problem with her parents," said Ms. Hawkins. "Her choices are very difficult."

I know about hard choices, Lan thought. *I've just made some myself. And I don't know yet how they'll turn out.*

The first choice had been his decision to leave the Havilands, where he had been staying with Jenny and her family, and to move into his own apartment. But that choice had involved an even more difficult decision: to finance the move he had had to sell the viola Lissa Mainzer had left him.

When she died four months earlier, Lissa had seemed to be Lan's only friend. But her suicide had been the motivation for forming the hotline, bringing together four kids who barely knew each other. The only thing that Jenny and Kurt, both seniors, and Angie, a junior like Lan, had in common then was that Lissa had left something precious to each of them. Since the four had banded together, determined to do whatever they could to keep anyone else from ever feeling as desperate as Lissa, the hotline had grown to

7

a group of thirteen. Some of them had become Lan's close friends.

Closest of all was probably April Cappelli, who smiled sympathetically and, to Lan's extreme self-consciousness, mouthed a kiss from across the room. Pretty April, short like him but round and curvy with dark eyes and a winning smile, she had arrived at the meeting a bit late, or he knew she'd be sitting right beside him. He smiled back and then looked away. He lowered his eyes, thinking about Star, and about the two who had died last night.

"Her choices are very difficult," Ms. Hawkins was saying, perched on the old desk in Temporary 3-A, her cranberry red skirt smoothed over her knees. Angie looked at her admiringly. This elegant black woman was definitely the best-dressed teacher at Roosevelt High School—all of her clothes were made of unusual fabrics that looked handwoven, like this wool skirt, or silks and linens with exotic African designs. And she was one of the best-liked teachers as well.

Difficult choices. Angie knew about those. Her thoughts spun back to a few weeks ago when it was Gillian Cole who had had to make a difficult choice, and Angie had become deeply involved in her decision. At the same time Angie had her own choice to make about Marcos Sanchez, the boy she had been going steady with for four years. "Life isn't simple and it isn't easy," her grandmother often said, and the longer Angie was on the hotline, the more she understood what Grandma meant.

"It sounds as though we have a lot to talk about today," the teacher was saying, her voice drawing Angie back to the present. "I know this tragic news about two students many of you knew is a hard way to begin

8

the new year. Still, I hope all of you had a good holiday break and are ready to get back to work."

"We had a fantastic vacation," Steven said. "We went back to Boston, where we used to live, and it was like visiting another planet. I'd forgotten how isolated and provincial it is here in Eldorado."

"*Provincial!*" Jenny sputtered. "I suppose you think we're all just a bunch of hicks!"

Ilana gave Steven a look of complete exasperation. "Of course not, Jenny," she said, soothingly. And to everyone, "Please try to overlook my brother's unfortunate lack of tact. Steven, your choice of words, as always, leaves a lot to be desired."

Mr. Montgomery stroked his bushy beard. "I'll bet a lot of us are from someplace else and chose Eldorado because it's special," he said diplomatically. "I know I did."

Angie secretly wondered if Steven was right. She had lived her whole life in this city and had no basis for comparison. Angie glanced around the room, trying to remember who was native and who had come from somewhere else. Lan, she knew, was a refugee from Vietnam; everyone had trouble with his family name, Nguyen, pronounced something like WING. He had lived in Eldorado for more than a couple of years—Angie wasn't sure exactly how many. Then there was Rob Saylor, who had come from California only a few months ago, and Jenny, whose family moved from Connecticut when she was in middle school, and Michelle Piper who had come here when her mother quit making TV movies and married Michelle's stepfather.

Angie's glance swept over Kurt Lundquist, a native, like her, but with a big difference: Kurt's father owned a European car agency, and his family lived in the exclusive part of town. Mr. Lundquist had recently been elected mayor; his swearing-in ceremony was only this past week. Angie wasn't sure if she should congratulate Kurt or not; there had been so much scandal surrounding the election, when it came out that Kurt's father had been having an affair with Michelle Piper's mother, that Angie felt too embarrassed to say anything. She wondered how Kurt felt about it. She felt awkward, and she wasn't even involved.

"I'm going to change the subject for a moment, if I may," Mr. Montgomery said, interrupting Angie's mental census-taking. "We've all got a lot on our minds today, but the beginning of a new year seems like a good time to look back over where we've been and then forward to where we're going, as a group. Does anyone want to start?"

Angie couldn't think of anything offhand, but wasn't surprised when Jenny plunged right in.

"I guess what really impresses me is what a solid group we've got. There's not only all of us who signed on at the beginning, but the newer ones—Nikki, Kristen, and Jason. So, Mr. Montgomery," Jenny said earnestly, "I'm looking forward to growing even more so we can help even more kids. Kids like Joseph DiAngelis. Maybe if he had called us we could have helped him."

"We're also getting lots more calls," Rob added. "From Roosevelt, and from other schools, too. I remember in the beginning when if we got one call in a three-hour shift, we were happy. I don't know what the average number of calls is now, but it's a lot more than it used to be."

"Right before Christmas I had six calls in one afternoon shift," Nikki Vavra reported. "Not all of them what you'd call crisis calls, though. And not all of them drug-related, although two were from people who wanted the number of a drug-treatment program—for 'friends,' they said. I tried to get them to talk, since I didn't really believe that stuff about the 'friends,' but they refused to discuss anything. Another call was from a girl who says she gets almost straight As, but it's the 'almost' that drives her parents crazy. Her father yells, 'Why can't you get all As like your brother?' and her mother blames it on the father, because he divorced her. She just needed somebody to talk to."

"Sounds like you had a busy shift, Nikki."

"It was. Actually, the hardest one was a kid who wanted to know what I thought he should get his girlfriend for Christmas, because if it wasn't the right thing she'd break up with him."

"Did she actually *say* she'd break up with him?" April Cappelli wanted to know. "Or was he just *afraid* she would?"

"Some of both," Nikki said. "She was dropping some pretty broad hints. So I said if he was really so worried about pleasing his girlfriend, maybe we should talk about their relationship. For about a half hour he talked and I listened, and then he thanked me about six times, because he said I'm the only person who's ever really listened to him! Actually the girl who called earlier said almost the same thing."

"I can relate to that," Kristen Hallett said. "It's unusual to find somebody who listens. Parents, for instance. Mine don't listen to me. Not really *listen*."

"Most don't, according to the calls I get," said Rob Saylor. He flashed Jenny a smile. "That's why the hotline is so important."

Angie silently agreed with Rob and with Kristen, a new hotliner whom she didn't know well. Angie still had not been able to talk much with anyone in her

11

family about what had really happened with her break-up with Marcos, because no one wanted to hear it—not her grandparents whom she lived with, not her divorced parents, not her married sister. Nobody.

Then April Cappelli brought up the subject of teachers who don't listen, and Ms. Hawkins said, "It *is* too bad that few people really listen, but think how lucky you all are to be aware of it and able to do something about it with the hotline."

We really are lucky, Angie mused. *I wonder if anybody ever listened to Karen and Joseph.*

Jenny was deep in thought about Mr. Montgomery's original question regarding where the hotline was going when Steven's voice caught her attention.

"It's a reflection of the stresses in our society," he was intoning pedantically. "The breakdown of the family. Increased pressure to succeed."

Jenny and Ilana both glared at Steven. Ilana's brother was, Jenny thought, one of the most pompous, arrogant, impossible people she knew. But in spite of all that he always seemed to understand exactly what was going on with the callers, even when they weren't clear about it themselves. Jenny worried, though, about how Steven came across to people who called in. He set Jenny's teeth on edge, so she could imagine the effect he'd have on a caller—*especially* somebody who had a problem with authority. Steven was "Authority" with a capital A.

Now's as good a time as any, Jenny decided, taking a deep breath. "That's why," she said aloud, "I'm wondering when we're going to expand the hotline hours. Three o'clock until six on school days just doesn't seem like enough. Especially at a crisis time like this, with two people dead."

12

"I know you'd like to go seven days a week, Jenny," Mr. Montgomery said, "and I know you want to reach more people, but we've still got the same problems."

"At least until nine o'clock," Jenny pleaded. "Ten or eleven would be better. We've got enough hotliners to do that now, if people are willing to take longer shifts and stay later."

"There's more to it than that, Jenny," Mr. Montgomery said patiently. "The school would have to pay a security guard overtime to keep the building open nights and weekends. There are considerations for your safety."

"I know." Jenny sighed. "But that's still my goal."

"Not a bad goal," Ms. Hawkins said. "Just unrealistic. Better to do a superb job in the hours we *do* operate than to spread ourselves too thin, don't you think?"

But before Jenny could frame a response, the phone rang in the small inner office, the first call of the day for the hotline. Jason Aragon, one of the newer hotliners, jumped up to answer. Ilana, his partner, was right behind him. There was no point in Jenny trying to pursue her argument when everyone was half waiting for Jason to come back and tell them about the call. She took advantage of the interruption and crossed the room to crouch next to Lan.

"You had a phone call last night," she whispered. "Adam Wolf wants you to call him this evening. Here's his number." Lan nodded his thanks and stuck the note in his shirt pocket. "You're coming over tonight, right?" Jenny continued. "You can ride home with me in the truck. We'll put your bike in the back, and I'll take you over to your place later, if you want me to."

"Okay," he said.

Jenny scooted back to her seat. She knew who

13

Adam Wolf was: the boy from the Youth Symphony who had bought Lissa's viola. She almost hated to give Lan the message. Jenny hadn't forgiven him for selling that viola. Or Adam for buying it. And all just so Lan could move into his own apartment.

Jason and Ilana returned from the inner office, looking puzzled. "A drug call," Jason reported. "No name. He said he's worried about his friend who's been getting high on his dad's asthma pills, and did we think that was dangerous. I said I was pretty sure it *was* dangerous, but just as I was starting to ask him some questions, he hung up. Like someone had walked into the room or something."

"I don't believe for one second it was about his *friend*," Ilana stated flatly. "He was calling about himself, I'll bet anything. But I wish he'd just come out and *say* that. It would be so much easier to help people if they were honest!"

Kurt stood up abruptly and began pacing around the hotline office, aware that people were watching him. He didn't care; he felt antsy. He had cut a class after lunch to rush downtown to the ceremony at City Hall when his father was sworn in as mayor. Everything had gone smoothly, but Kurt was wary, on guard against the unexpected, remembering the horrible publicity at the time of the election. And then this news about Karen and Joseph. He had known Karen slightly, a quiet, studious girl, and Joseph had been a hotshot basketball player with scholarship offers from major universities. *How sad*, Kurt thought. *Two lives over almost before they've begun.*

The Duck, due any minute, always made Kurt uneasy. The vice principal had once seemed to Kurt like the archfiend, the enemy of the hotline, committed to its failure. And it was because of one of the Duck's major rules—not to get personally involved with any of the callers—that Kurt had ended up temporarily suspended from the hotline. Kurt felt he'd relax only after the Duck's visit was over.

Mr. Duckworth arrived at last, snowflakes melting on his coat collar. Kurt stopped pacing and leaned against the wall.

"Well, well, well," the Duck began, rubbing his hands. "Happy New Year to all of you. It looks as though the hotline is off to a fine start after the holidays." He pulled an envelope from his pocket. "I have something here to share with you."

The Duck read a short note from a parent, unnamed, thanking the hotline for being so helpful to his daughter. As a result of some hotliner's skillful conversation, the whole family was now getting counseling, and everything was going better.

"That's the good news," Mr. Duckworth said somberly. "But there's something else I need to talk with all of you about. You've probably heard that we lost two members of our student body last night in separate tragedies. We've learned that Karen Garcia was driving home from a friend's house early in the evening when her car was struck head-on by a pickup truck. The driver of the truck was drunk. Karen, one of our honor students, died on the way to the hospital. Sometime later, Joseph DiAngelis, a promising young athlete, died of an accidental drug overdose."

The hotliners waited in respectful silence.

"You may be getting some calls about these tragedies," Mr. Duckworth went on. "And I count on you to handle those calls to the best of your ability. It's upsetting to everyone when something like this happens, and it's worse when it is someone you know well.

15

I have no other details, but if I learn anything that might be helpful, I'll pass it on through your advisors. So there you are," he concluded. "Keep up the good work." He waggled his fingers in farewell and left.

Kurt slid back into his seat. *The Duck's not such a bad guy,* Kurt thought, *even though everyone still jokes about his tight jackets and fuzzy bald head; he really does support the hotline after all.*

Lan put a couple of chickens into the Havilands' oven and began to peel a pile of raw shrimp. The shrimp was for a quick stir-fry for tonight's dinner. Later he would dress up the chickens with some sauces—a curry, maybe, and something Italian—and pack them in the freezer for future meals. He liked doing this kind of work; it helped him get his head straight.

He was relieved that Jenny was in her room, leaving him alone in the kitchen. He knew she thought he was making a big mistake, moving to his own apartment. She didn't understand that it was his only real option. He had been thinking about it for a long time. It was his duty to provide a place for his sister, Sieu An, and her son, Johnny, some safe place for them to get away from her husband's violent temper.

But even if he hadn't felt he had to take care of his family, Lan knew he couldn't go on living with the Havilands. It felt too much like charity, even though Lan did what he could, mainly cooking for them, to help pay his way. It was just as well. Mr. Haviland was a brilliant history professor and a keen chess player, but he didn't know a spatula from a paring knife. Ms. Moore-Haviland was too busy going to law school to remember what, if anything, was in the refrigerator, let alone to put a meal on the table. And Jenny managed to combine the worst culinary traits of both; she was a lot like her parents. Lan felt better cooking, anyway—it made him feel like he was earning his keep.

The Havilands had been nice to him, tried to make him feel like part of the family. It had been a long time since Lan had had any kind of father or mother in his life—not since he had last seen his own father in Vietnam eight years before. And he had dreaded telling the Havilands his plans to move as much as he would have dreaded telling his own parents something he knew would displease them.

It was Ms. Moore-Haviland who asked the first tough question when Lan told them his decision. "Is your sister divorcing her husband? That must be very difficult for her, with the little boy. I hope she's getting good legal advice."

Then Mr. Haviland voiced his concern: "It's none of my business," he said, "but apartments cost money. Are you sure you can swing it with what you earn at Red's?"

Lan had explained the difficult decision he had made, one of the hardest of his life: quitting the Youth Symphony, which he could no longer afford time for, and selling his beloved viola to get the money for the deposit on the apartment.

But it wasn't just the senior Havilands who asked hard questions; Jenny had come completely unglued. "How could you *do* that!" she said, her blue eyes wide with astonishment. "It was *Lissa's* viola! She wanted you to have it because you're a talented musician, not to rent some apartment, when you don't even have to do it!" Lan saw that she was close to tears.

"But I feel I do have to do it," Lan answered calmly.

"Now, Jenny," her mother had interrupted gently.

"But, Mom, can't we do something?" Jenny per-

17

sisted. "Can't we buy the viola from him, so at least it doesn't go to strangers?"

"It's not going to a stranger," Lan had said quickly. "I sold it to another violist in the Youth Symphony. He knew Lissa, too. He admired her a lot. And he told me about a month ago that if I ever wanted to sell it, he'd give me a good price for it. He even said I could borrow it sometimes if I wanted to."

"Who is it?" Jenny asked darkly.

"Adam Wolf. He's a senior at Arts and Science Academy. Maybe you met him when you and Rob came to take pictures at our December concert."

"I don't remember any Adam Wolf," she said sourly. "Academy? Rich kid, huh?"

"I don't know if he's rich or not," Lan said, "but he's paying me two thousand dollars for it, plus his old viola. And I really need the money."

Lan knew that didn't satisfy her, but it was the best he could do. Suddenly Jenny's mother, trying to be helpful, had an inspiration: "Tell you what, Lan—if you'll come back and cook for us one night a week, we'll pay you double what Red's Diner pays. We could really use your excellent chef services, plus that way we'll get to see you, too."

"You'll be keeping a deserving family from almost certain starvation," Mr. Haviland said with a wistful smile. "But I want you to know that the thing I'll miss the most is our chess games."

"While I'm here I could also fix some meals for you to keep in the freezer and heat up in the microwave," Lan had responded thoughtfully, adding, "And maybe there will be time for chess," although he didn't really think there would be. Then they had all shaken hands and wished him luck—even Jenny. But he sensed that Jenny was still upset.

The one person who wholeheartedly approved of Lan's decision was April Cappelli. "Great, Lan!" she said when he told her. "Now we have a place to hang out. To be alone together." She had looked at him meaningfully when she said this. He had been to her apartment a few times since they had started spending time with each other, but only when her father was out. If Mr. Cappelli was at home, April wouldn't invite Lan to come in. "My dad is kind of strange," is all she would say.

April had wanted to come over to his apartment right away, but Lan put her off. "Let me get moved in first," he told her. "I don't want you to see it 'til it's fixed up."

"Then we can celebrate—maybe with some champagne?" she had teased him, but he shook his head. Twice now she had mysteriously produced bottles of champagne, and he had felt completely wasted at the time and wretched a few hours later. There wasn't going to be a third time; he didn't like feeling out of control, and he had made up his mind that alcohol and drugs were never going to be part of his life.

While the chickens were roasting, Lan took a minute to slip into Mr. Haviland's study to phone Adam Wolf.

"I've got some money for you," Adam said in his husky voice. "Do you want to meet me somewhere this evening?"

This evening? It was cold and windy with occasional blasts of stinging snow, nasty weather to be out riding a bike, and he didn't want to ask Jenny to give him a ride—she'd be curious about where he was going, curious about Adam, maybe even asking to meet the person who had bought the viola. Lan didn't want to have to deal with any of that. On the other hand, Lan was anxious to collect the money Adam owed him. It would make him feel a lot more secure. He'd do the bike ride.

"Okay," Lan agreed. "Nine o'clock, at Red's Diner."

During dinner Mr. Haviland began to tell them about the historical project he was working on at the university to commemorate the five-hundredth anniversary of Columbus's discovery of America. But Jenny was distracted; she wanted to talk about Karen Garcia and Joseph DiAngelis.

"Did you know them?" Ms. Haviland-Moore asked.

"Not well," Jenny said. "But I know who they are. *Were*. It's just so awful to think that yesterday this time they were probably eating dinner, just the way we are, and a couple of hours later they were dead!"

"What happened?" Mr. Haviland asked. "Do you know?"

Jenny passed on the information Mr. Duckworth had given them. "That's all I've heard," she said. "What about you, Lan?"

Lan shook his head. "All I know," he replied, his jaw tense, "is, it never should have happened. Like you said at the meeting today, Jenny, none of it *would* have happened if it hadn't been for alcohol and drugs."

For the rest of the meal, the Havilands talked about the two tragedies. Jenny didn't mention Lissa, but Lan knew she must have been thinking of her, as he was.

Lan listened attentively, but he was aware that time was passing, that he still had to finish up here and then ride all the way to Red's. At last he managed to get away, turning down their inevitable offers to take him in the truck.

"You are so stubborn!" Jenny had called after him in exasperation as he pedaled away.

As it turned out Lan had to wait almost a half hour

for Adam to show up. Fortunately, he had his physics book with him, so he could study while he waited. He was deep into the properties of light when Adam slid into the seat opposite him. "Sorry I'm late, Lan," he said. Adam set his motorcycle helmet on the table and unzipped his black leather jacket. "Cold out there."

Adam was tall and lanky with long arms and legs, big hands, and long, strong fingers. His dark brown hair fell over his forehead, his mouth was straight and serious, but his blue eyes shone with good humor. His ruggedly handsome face was red from the cold.

"You rode your motorcycle?" Lan asked.

"Yeah. My brother needed the Jeep. I don't even want to think about what the windchill factor is. Maybe some coffee will thaw me out."

Adam kept up a line of inconsequential talk until two steaming mugs were set in front of them. Lan wanted to ask how Adam was doing with the viola, but he kept silent. The truth was that Lan didn't think Adam was much of a violist. It bothered him a little that a person with such mediocre talent would be using the fine instrument that had been Lissa's pride and joy and that he, Lan, had loved to play. He missed the viola almost as though it were a real person, and at that moment he suffered a pang of regret and longing that became a deeper pang of missing Lissa.

But Lan tried not to think about that now—the decision was made and the deal was done; Adam had the viola, Lan had collected a thousand dollars, and tonight Adam was going to give him the remaining thousand dollars.

Adam stirred milk and sugar into his coffee. "Listen, Lan," he said finally. "I hate to tell you this, but I don't have the grand I owe you. The best I can do right now is two hundred, and I'll get the rest for you as soon as I can. That's why I'm late—I hated to keep you waiting, but I was trying to get the rest, and I couldn't. I hope that doesn't mess things up for you too much." Adam pulled a wad of twenties out of his wallet, fanned them out on the table, and then collapsed the fan and shoved the pile toward Lan.

Lan studied the pile of money in silence. "When will you have the rest?" he asked finally.

Adam looked away. "See, my brother is giving it to me, but he's short on cash right now. He says he'll have it in the next few weeks."

Lan said nothing, but his disappointment must have shown.

"Maybe sooner. Honest, Lan, I'm sorry about this, but there's not a damned thing I can do. Nathaniel is being really nice to buy me the viola in the first place, and if he says he'll do it, then he'll do it. He's good for the money. It's just that these things happen. You have to trust me. I know my brother will come through. He's never let me down. I don't think he'd ever let anybody down. You can think of it as money in the bank, really."

"All right," Lan said, folding the bills and tucking them into his pocket. He hadn't figured on this. He had a few hundred dollars in a savings account that he had managed to put away a little at a time from each week's paycheck, but he needed more if he was going to be able to make it—cover rent and utilities, buy food, pay for his lunches at school, plus all the incidentals. Even stuff like toothpaste cost money. Which reminded him—he needed to see a dentist. One of his back molars was beginning to bother him.

As soon as Sieu An and Johnny came to live with him, Lan reasoned, things would get better. Sieu An could get a part-time job and contribute to the rent and food. Maybe next year when Johnny started school, she could work full-time. He figured he could make it for six months without her help; by that time, he was certain, they would be sharing expenses. And it would be summer and he'd get a full-time job and start saving seriously for his future.

But at this moment Lan's future seemed cloudy. Only his past remained vivid: a young boy, running across a beach in Vietnam towards the rickety old boat that was to take him to freedom. The same boy on the refugee boat, separated from his sister, their older brother killed, their little brother dead from thirst. Later, when he and his sister had been miraculously reunited, that young boy had sworn a solemn vow that he would someday work to relieve human suffering, to do all he could to heal sickness and save lives. He would become a doctor.

But it was one thing to make that vow, and now it was something else to make the vow a reality. That's when the clouds rolled in. His sister had married an American, Wayne Troxler, and the couple had opened a Vietnamese restaurant. They worked hard, and Lan had worked with them until Wayne's volatile temper had come between them. Lan knew that he was not the only target of that temper. He worried about his sister and her son. Sieu An denied that Wayne ever struck them, but Lan had seen suspicious bruises on her arms and the fear in Johnny's eyes. Lan had to get them away from the violence.

Like that vow, that was easier said than done. It seemed to Lan that no matter how many hours he worked, he was always on the stark edge of survival. He never begrudged Kurt his luxurious lifestyle, with a hot sports car and glamorous ski vacations, or Jenny the security of knowing she could go to whatever college she chose. He didn't envy his friends from modest family backgrounds like Angie and April, although it seemed likely to Lan that they would be able to realize their dreams, if they were willing to work hard. But even they were well-off compared to Lan. And medical school was something else—years and years of expensive training. How was he going to make that happen, especially with his family responsibilities?

The only thing Lan had of value was the viola Lissa had left him. He had decided, painfully, after long consideration, that he would have to give it up in order to take care of his sister. Where that decision might leave him later on when he'd finished high school, he just didn't know. If he assumed responsibility for his sister and nephew, would he still be able to go on to college and then medical school? Could he ever afford to? His dream of becoming a doctor, of helping humanity, would have to take second place to his duty to his family. He needed the money to do that. The viola would have to be sacrificed. But not the dream. He was not going to let go of the dream.

But now Adam Wolf sat across from him in his expensive motorcycle leathers and explained, frowning with concern, that he could give him only part of the money, and he wasn't sure when the rest would come along.

"It's okay," Lan said.

"I'm really sorry, Lan. I hope this doesn't make things hard for you."

"Don't worry about it. Like you said, it's money in the bank, there for later."

"Right. The viola's a beauty," Adam said with a disarming grin. "It's got the best tone I've ever heard. You doing okay with my old one?"

Lan smiled faintly. "It plays. *You* know."

24

"Yeah, I know." Adam nervously drummed his long fingers on the table top. "Listen, Lan, I was wondering something. I almost hate to ask you this, but what the hell."

"Yes?" Lan waited.

"Well, the thing is, Lan, you're a much better violist than I'll ever be, even if I practiced twenty hours a day, which I don't. Sometimes twenty *minutes* seems like a lot, with everything else going on. You know how it is."

Lan nodded, waiting for Adam to get to the point.

"You're going to think this is really crazy, Lan. But I was wondering if you'd sort of, you know, *coach* me. Practice with me. Because I got a note from Mr. Ellis saying I'm on probation with the Youth Symphony. I have to reaudition in a few weeks if I want to stay in the orchestra. I like playing, but I'm not that good— not like you. So I'm wondering if you'd work with me for maybe an hour a couple times a week, any time you say. I'd pay you," he added hastily.

Lan thought about it. It would be a lot of extra work. He really didn't know how he'd fit it all in.

"Does ten dollars an hour sound okay?" Adam continued hurriedly. "You could come to our house, maybe stay for dinner. My mom would like that. Or I could come to your place, if that works out better for you."

Ten dollars an hour was a lot more than Red's was paying. Lan made up his mind. "All right."

A relieved smile spread across Adam's face. "When can we start?"

Lan explained what his life was like—working at Red's, cooking for Jenny's family, his commitment to the hotline. "I also have a girlfriend," he added in a low voice.

25

"Jeez, man, when do you get a chance to see her?"

"I don't, very much. I guess I could spend a couple of hours a week with you after school, until your audition."

Adam grinned at him. "Lan, you're saving my life."

"I'm glad to be able to help you," Lan replied seriously.

Brenda, the waitress, came by their table to offer more coffee. Lan was anxious to start his trip home, but Adam accepted a refill, and out of politeness Lan did, too.

"Listen, what's this hotline all about?" Adam asked, changing the subject. "I think you mentioned it at rehearsal once."

Lan explained—how it had gotten started after Lissa's death, how it operated. "We had some problems at first. Getting approval from the school, going through training, and then spreading the word so people know we're there. But we're getting lots of calls now."

"It sure sounds like a good idea," Adam said thoughtfully. "Do you get a lot of calls from kids who're actually thinking of killing themselves?"

"No, but just about everything else you can think of." Lan described their meetings and the kinds of calls they discussed. He talked about Karen and Joseph and how the hotline expected to get calls from people upset by the senseless deaths. "Talking won't change what happened," Lan said, "but it does seem to help how people feel about it."

"We could sure use something like that at Academy," Adam said. "I know a lot of kids who really need to talk to somebody."

Lan was struck by Adam's sincerity. He seemed genuinely interested in the hotline. "So why don't you

26

start one? I could tell you how we did it, the steps we went through."

"Would you? That would be great!" He began to zip up his leather suit, and Lan reached for his thin jacket.

Pedaling back to his apartment against a frigid headwind, Lan wondered what he was getting into, agreeing to tutor this boy who seemed to have everything going for him, except musical talent. It was beginning to feel more and more like overload.

Thursday, January 4

"**H**ello," Kurt said, unfolding his long legs and reaching for his note pad, "this is Ears, the High School Hotline." Nikki Vavra, his shift partner, closed her biology book and looked up expectantly.

"Uh, you're going to have to explain this to me," said the boy on the other end of the line. "I'm not sure how this hotline thing works."

"It's simple—you tell me what you'd like to talk about, and I listen. Then we can discuss it if you want to."

"Do I have to give you my name?"

"Not if you don't want to. But it's better if you give me something I can call you."

There was a long pause. "Ninja," the boy said finally. "Yeah, just call me Ninja."

That's a strange one, Kurt thought; are we dealing with a mutant turtle or a Japanese assassin? But he said, "Okay, Ninja. Now how can we help you?"

"It's kind of a long story. My family—well, it's not in the best shape. Everybody thinks it's great, but it isn't at all. Nobody would ever guess it's the mess it is."

I can relate to that, Kurt thought; *if I didn't know*

28

better, I'd think he was talking about my family. Aloud he said, "Sounds like you have some trouble with your family."

"I guess you could say that," Ninja said dryly. "Everybody thinks my parents are the perfect couple, but they fight all the time. When my dad bothers to come home at all, that is. I have two brothers. My older brother moved out and got his own apartment, and he says I can move in with him, which I want to do, except we've got this younger brother, and I can't take him with me and I can't leave him behind."

"Sounds tough," Kurt said, trying to draw his caller out a little more.

"Yeah, well, it is. You know, it's not so great at home, but I'm not so sure it would be better with my brother," Ninja said, abruptly falling silent.

"It sounds like you like your brother, but you're not sure you want to live with him," Kurt said cautiously.

"I worry about him," Ninja said slowly. "I think he's into some things he shouldn't be into."

"Like what?"

Silence. Kurt let it stretch between them, as he had been trained to do, letting Ninja figure out how to say whatever was so hard. "Drugs," he blurted out.

"Using?"

"Yeah. Cocaine. But that's not all."

"What else?"

"I think he's dealing, too."

"What makes you think your brother is into drugs?"

"Well, he *acts* different. He dropped out of school, and my parents don't even know. They think he's still a junior at the university, and I know he hardly went at all last semester. He's got this trust fund that he's supposed to use to pay for his education, so all the bills go directly to him. And he doesn't live at home any-

29

more, so my parents don't have a clue. It's easy to make them believe anything."

"How do you know he's dealing?"

"Money, mostly. He doesn't have a job, as far as I know, but sometimes he has a lot of money, I mean a *whole* lot, and other times he's kind of broke. Then the next time you see him he's rich again. My parents don't know about that part. They think he's invested his trust fund somehow, and that's why he has lots of extra cash. He's like that." Ninja laughed bitterly. "Once when he was in high school he bought this table at a garage sale for five dollars. Then he fixed it up and sold it to an antique dealer for *five hundred*. I guess he's always been good at buying and selling."

"But you're sure it's drugs now?" Kurt prompted.

Ninja sighed. "Yeah. I'm sure. Sometimes he buys stuff—things, I mean, not drugs—for me and my brother. My parents don't have any idea what kind of money he must spend, but I do. And he buys us expensive stuff. My little brother's twelve, and he worships my older brother like he's a god or something. I can't tell him what my brother's really into." Ninja took a deep ragged breath. "It feels like the whole world is falling apart around me, and I don't know how to stop it." His voice dropped so low that Kurt had to strain to catch his words.

"Does your brother know that *you* know what he's doing?" Kurt asked.

"Yeah. But we don't talk about it anymore," Ninja said.

"What would happen if you just leveled with him? Told him you know he's into some highly dangerous stuff and you're scared about what's going to happen to him?"

"I did that. He went into this total rage. I never saw him like that before—completely out of control. He

30

kept insisting there's no problem, and I kept saying, 'But there *is* a problem—look at yourself!' and he'd scream no there wasn't, it was all *me*. And he started calling me names, and then I got scared and shut up. I don't know what to do, but I can't just let it go. Can I?"

"No," Kurt said carefully, "I don't think you can just let it go." He thought of Star, the girl who talked to Lan about her parents growing marijuana; how worried she was, and how worried Ninja seemed to be. *People doing drugs just don't realize how it affects the people who care about them,* Kurt thought.

"What's your name?" Ninja asked abruptly.

"Kurt."

"Look, Kurt, I don't like what my brother's doing. He could get hurt, maybe killed. He could get busted and end up in jail. What he's doing is really wrong. But he's my brother, and I love him. I don't know what to do."

Kurt struggled to find the right thing to say. "Maybe," he said tentatively, "you need to look at your part in your brother's problem. You said he buys you things. Maybe you could refuse to accept whatever he buys you. And get your little brother to do the same, if you can do that without telling him why. That would send your older brother a pretty powerful message about how you feel. It's just an idea. I can't tell you what to do, Ninja. Nobody can."

"Thanks," Ninja said. "I—I . . . Well, thanks, that's all."

Kurt hung up the phone and stared at it.

"That sounded like a hard one," Nikki said.

"Yeah. The kind I don't like. This guy's brother uses drugs and deals them, too. Another of your all-American royally screwed-up families." He filled Nikki in on the details. "I'm glad it's not my decision."

31

"Speaking of screwed-up families . . ." Nikki trailed off.

"What?" Kurt tensed; was this going to be a question about *his* screwed-up family?

"I'm thinking of Michelle," Nikki explained. "Have you spent any time with her lately?"

Kurt was relieved that the question wasn't too close to home. He and Nikki had grown up together, friends since her mother had gone to work for his father when they were both little kids. But he still didn't like to discuss his family with her. He wondered why she was asking him about Michelle; he and Michelle had dated off and on, but that had started to unravel when he had developed a crush on Michelle's mother, and it had fallen apart completely when rumors of their parents' affair became public. Since then, he and Michelle had managed to establish a distant friendship, nothing more. "Not much," he answered carefully. "Michelle went with her mother to their condo to ski over Christmas. She's been spending more time with her mom since the Pipers separated. Why?"

"I know she's going through a tough time, but she looks really *bad*. She's lost a lot of weight. I was noticing yesterday at the hotline meeting. I thought you might know if she's been sick or something."

Kurt shook his head. "I don't think she's been sick, but she did say she's been on some kind of killer diet."

"But all that weight she's lost—it can't be healthy."

It was a response Kurt expected from Nikki, a lean, well-toned athlete. "I agree with you, but she's going to modeling school, and they told her when she started at the school that she needed to lose twenty pounds. The camera makes you look fat or something." He shrugged. "Anyway, she's been living on

32

about eleven strands of spaghetti with tomato juice for the last six weeks."

"She must feel starved most of the time."

"Not starved, but definitely hyper. I promised I wouldn't talk about this, but she's taking her mother's diet pills."

"Oh, Kurt, that's awful! Those things are terrible! Can't you get her to quit?"

"She wants to be thin. The school tells her she has to be. What can I do? I'm hoping that when she makes the twenty-pound goal she'll be satisfied and stop."

"I hope so, too. Michelle's really beautiful. It would be a shame for her to starve herself so that she looks more like a scarecrow than a fashion model."

The phone rang and Kurt took the call, a girl fighting with her parents about the age of the boy she was dating. She was fourteen, she said. The boyfriend? Twenty-two. Kurt settled back to listen. The girl, mouthy and rebellious, reminded him of his sister, Dana.

Angie sat impatiently in a booth at Popeye's, the after-school hangout, watching the clock. The minute hand moved around slowly as she sipped her soft drink. She had found a note in her locker from Cathy and Lily, inviting her to meet them there. Angie was glad to do it; she hadn't seen much of the two girls in a long time.

Cathy and Lily both went out with boys who were buddies of Marcos, and they had been shocked when Angie broke up with him over a month ago. At first they didn't believe her—they could not accept that she had broken off with the boy she had been going with since junior high, more than four years. They had even tried to set up traps so that she'd have to run into Marcos.

Being without Marcos had been hard for a while. Angie had to admit to herself that she hadn't felt so glad it was over on New Year's Eve, when everyone she knew was with *someone*. At Christmas Jack Mertz had sent her a fuzzy stuffed bear holding a scrap of paper with a poem printed in tiny letters: "Roses are red/But this bear will be blue/If we can't ring in/The New Year with YOU." It was signed, "Jack, the Bear."

It made her laugh, but dear as Jack was, Angie didn't want to spend New Year's Eve with him. That evening was too special to spend with someone who wasn't special to her, at least not in the way Jack wanted to be. To make sure she had an excuse, Angie offered to baby-sit with her brand-new nephew so that Terry and her husband, Jimmy, could go out and visit friends for a while. The baby had screamed nonstop until just before Terry returned, alone and furious, hours later than she had promised. Jimmy had been picked up on a DWI and hauled off to the drunk tank at the county jail.

"I told him and told him," Terry had wailed, "but no, he had to have one more beer, and then another one. And I said, let me drive, but he wouldn't. Then we get stopped at a road block, and my big macho husband registers 0.12 on the blood alcohol test, three points over the legal limit. And they take us down to the jail and book him and throw him in the drunk tank with all these other guys. I've never been so embarrassed in my life."

Angie didn't say anything, but she put her arm around her sister and held her comfortingly while Terry cried. "Was the baby good?" Terry asked after a while, peering into the cradle.

34

"Pretty good," Angie said wearily.

Angie had spent the rest of the night on her sister's sofa, so tired she fell asleep instantly, and when the baby cried again, Angie let her sister get up and take care of him.

Now Cathy and Lily rushed in, out of breath, and waved at her. They ordered drinks at the counter, brought them to Angie's booth, and for a while they chatted about movies they had seen, sexy TV stars they admired, clothes and jewelry they had bought or wanted to buy. Angie found herself growing slightly bored.

Then the two girls got down to the real reason for the meeting. "There's something you ought to know, Angie," Cathy began. "And we thought it was better if we told you before you heard it from somebody else."

"Have you seen Marcos lately?" Lily asked darkly.

"No, I haven't, as a matter-of-fact." Angie saw Lily and Cathy exchange glances. "Why?" she asked.

Lily leaned close. "He has a new girlfriend," she said, her eyes intent on Angie.

Angie hadn't expected that, and for a second she was afraid her surprise showed too plainly, more like shock. Well, she was kind of shocked—it hadn't been that long since they broke up. Angie decided not to say anything but to wait for them to tell her whatever it was they wanted her to know.

"Her name is Hope Vargas. She goes to St. Jerome's." When Angie didn't respond, Cathy rushed on. "They were at a New Year's Eve party together. I hear it's pretty serious."

Pretty serious? How could it be "pretty serious" so soon? Angie wondered, still saying nothing.

"I hear he's even planning to give her a ring. Or maybe he's already given it to her."

Ring? Surely not the ring he had given Angie for

35

her birthday as an engagement ring, and that she had given back to him? She felt herself getting angry: so this is how much he had loved her, that it had taken him only six weeks to find somebody else to be in love with, and he had given the ring to her!

But she had to say something to Lily and Cathy, watching her like a pair of hawks. "Well, good for him, and good for her, too. I think it's terrific that Marcos has somebody new." She hoped she sounded convincing, because it still hurt, a little. Even when it was completely over, the way it was with her and Marcos, it was hard. There were still memories, still feelings.

"You don't sound very upset about it," Cathy commented. "It almost sounds like you didn't love him very much."

"But Marcos is the one who rushed off and found somebody new!" Angie protested.

"To tell you the truth," Lily confided, "I'm not sure he's really as much in love with Hope as he makes out. I think he still loves you. I think you could have him back like this"—she snapped her fingers—"if you wanted him. And we'd be real happy if you did. Hope isn't all that great, if you want to know. It was much more fun with you, Angie."

"Well, thanks," Angie said. "But the thing is, I'm not in love with Marcos. I was once, but not anymore. It's really, really over." Angie stood up and began buttoning her coat. "Thanks for telling me. Give them my best, okay?"

I wasn't lying, she thought to herself as she hurried home, her hands shoved deep in her pockets; *it really is over*. And probably with Cathy and Lily, too. Angie realized that without Marcos, she no longer had anything in common with them. Now when she thought of friends, it was the hotliners who came to mind.

Jenny and Rob spread out the photographs on the floor of the solar room. This had been Lan's room for weeks, and now it was just an ordinary room again. The whole house seemed suddenly different without Lan here. In a way it was good to have the space again, but in other ways it seemed strangely empty. Jenny knew that her parents missed him, too. Even the two dachshunds, Hansel and Gretel, seemed lost. Lan was the one who took them out for their evening walks most of the time, when everybody else was too busy. Jenny was surprised to realize how much her family had come to rely on Lan.

Rob lined up the pictures they had settled on, and Jenny arranged her captions under them. The project had started as a photo essay on the Eldorado Youth Symphony for the *Blue & Gold*, the school paper. Rob had taken the photographs at the concert in December, and Jenny had interviewed a number of musicians. But after the story ran in the *B&G*, Jenny's mother suggested taking the idea in expanded form to the local newspaper. The *Tribune* editor seemed interested and suggested that with a different angle it might make a good feature for the "Living" section. Jenny was ecstatic. The deadline was the next afternoon, Friday, and they were still making last-minute changes.

"It's hard to make a final pick," Jenny complained.

Rob grinned. "I took three rolls. There ought to be *some* good ones."

"That's the problem. They're *all* good."

Rob had begun with a shot of Lan leaving the house on his bicycle, dressed up in his black pants and white shirt, his viola strapped to his back. Then Jenny and Rob sped to the concert hall, where Lan had introduced them to other musicians and made it easier for

37

them to slip around unnoticed. They tried to capture the musicians' before-concert nervousness, the intense concentration of the performance, and the letdown afterward.

Rob, Jenny observed admiringly, was an ace at keeping his camera unobtrusive. He'd start talking to somebody, and part way through the conversation he'd ask, "Mind if I take a couple of shots?" and then snap them off so casually that the person didn't get tense or self-conscious. Jenny wished she was half as casual with her miniature tape recorder.

Now Jenny picked up a shot of Lan tuning his viola. Looking at the picture, she got angry with him all over again. "I can't believe he actually sold Lissa's viola!" she exclaimed.

"It's not Lissa's viola," Rob said calmly. "It's Lan's viola. She gave it to him, so it's his. And what he does with it is his business. You think Lissa is up in heaven somewhere looking down and saying, 'How come you sold *my* viola, Lan?'"

"No, of course not," Jenny replied, "but I'd think it would be important to him exactly because she gave it to him. If you gave me a present, I certainly wouldn't turn around and sell it."

"You would if you had to. And if you didn't do something you really needed to do because you were being sentimental, I'd be mad."

"I still don't understand why he thought he *had* to do it," Jenny grumbled. "Lan could have stayed as long as he wanted to at our house. It saved him a lot of money, living with us. He cooked most of our meals for us, but he didn't even have to do that."

"Maybe it's a matter of pride. Lan probably felt like a charity case. Maybe he just wants to be on his own, Jenny. How long did he stay with you?"

38

Jenny mentally went back over the series of events. It was almost exactly four months ago that her best friend, Lissa Mainzer, had committed suicide. The night she died, Lissa had written notes leaving gifts to four of her friends: Jenny, Kurt, Angie, and Lan, four people who scarcely knew each other until Lissa's death brought them together. Within a few weeks they had formed Ears, the High School Hotline.

Soon after the hotline was launched, Jenny had gotten a call from Lan, asking her to come and pick him up at the Saigon Café.

"I think it was toward the end of September," Jenny told Rob. "Lan wasn't getting along with his brother-in-law. His sister and her husband run a restaurant, and Lan used to live in this little storeroom next to the kitchen, until Wayne threw him out. When I went to get him, Lan was standing out in the alley with cartons of books and clothes and the viola. He said he was going to the Salvation Army, but I don't think he really knew what he was going to do. My parents invited him to stay with us, and he's been here ever since, until last weekend."

"All that happened before you and I found each other?"

Jenny grinned at Rob. "Sort of. I'd found you, but you hadn't found me yet."

"You're wrong—I found you first," he said, reaching over and rubbing the back of her neck. She wanted to *purr* when he touched her like that.

"You did not! Anyway," Jenny went on, "about a week ago, in the middle of dinner, Lan says something like, 'I've found an apartment and I'm moving out. Thank you all for your kindness.'"

"Did he explain why?"

"He says he has to take care of his sister and her

39

little boy, and that he couldn't tell us any more than that. And with Lan, you don't push. He's not exactly secretive, but he is very private. The weird thing is, a month ago it was really getting on my nerves having him around, and I thought he'd never leave. Now I'm really sorry he's gone. He's so quiet, he never talked that much, but it really left a hole in our family when he left."

Rob picked up one of the discarded photographs. "Who's this guy next to Lan?" he asked. "Do you know him, Jenny?"

Jenny studied the print. "Huh-uh. I guess we could ask Lan."

"Wait a minute—I got everybody to sign releases at the time, so I should be able to figure it out." Rob flipped through a folder full of forms. "I think that is Adam Wolf."

"Oh ho!" Jenny exclaimed, seizing the photograph. "So that's Adam Wolf!"

"What about him?"

"He's the guy who bought Lissa's viola. Okay, okay, *Lan's* viola. I wondered about him."

"Why wonder?"

"Who he is, that's all. Just curious."

Rob grabbed Jenny's hand. "That's what makes you such a good journalist. You are the most curious person I've ever met. It could get you into a lot of trouble. But it could also make you very successful and very famous."

She grinned at him. What an amazing human being this Rob Saylor was! She had never imagined she'd ever feel so totally comfortable with a boy, so completely at ease. And, she was convinced, so much in love. It still seemed incredible to her that somebody as

40

good-looking as Rob, with that striking white streak in his dark hair, could be attracted to plain old Jenny.

Rob grinned back, and Jenny leaned over and wound her arms around his neck. They kissed, and Jenny felt as though she was going to melt completely.

When they finally drew apart, Rob looked into her eyes. "Change your mind yet?" he asked softly.

"Nope," she said, trying to sound convincing. "Not until we've known each other for a full year."

"Starting from when?"

"From the first day I saw you at the first hotline meeting."

"That was in September! You want to wait until *next* September to make love? Think how old we'll be! We'll be going to college. Think of all that can happen between now and then."

"I'm thinking," she said stubbornly. "And it will be only good things that happen. We won't let it be any other way." She leaned toward him for another kiss.

"By the way," he said, "did I tell you my parents are leaving Sunday for Los Angeles? They'll be gone all week." He leered at Jenny and pretended to tap the ashes off an imaginary cigar. "That means I'll be out there all-l-l alone. Care to step into my parlor, my little chickadee?" he said. "You have nothing to fear, my dear. Trust me!"

"Trust you? Hah! You can turn off that leer. Nothing will sway me from my vow."

"Ah, you're a hard woman, Jennifer Haviland," he teased. "And that's why I'm crazy in love with you."

Jenny felt the warm familiar glow. "Oh, Rob . . ." she began and kissed him again, wondering how she was ever going to keep her promise to herself from now until September. Eight more months.

41

* * *

"It's better if you come to my place," Lan had told Adam Wolf, "than if I go to yours. At least the first time. You have better transportation than I do. And there won't be any distractions—nobody will be around at my apartment."

Lan liked being able to say that: *my apartment.*

Adam had agreed to Lan's suggestion. "Tell me how to get there and when you want me to come."

They agreed on a time: right after school twice a week, for an hour, before Lan took off for Red's. It would be tight, but he could manage, Lan was sure. And it wouldn't be for long—only until Adam got through the reaudition.

Once Lan had decided he must leave the Havilands', it had turned out to be harder than he imagined to find a cheap, furnished, one-bedroom apartment. Lan had settled for this one, with gold-colored carpet, stained and dirty, and a gaudy, green-flowered sofa and chair in the living room. The sofa sagged uncomfortably. There were no extra tables and no lamps, just the bare bulbs of the overhead fixtures. The yellow walls had faded to a dull, sickly color.

The cramped bedroom held a bed in not much better shape than the sofa. A couple of knobs were missing from the dresser, and one of the drawer fronts was completely gone. The bedroom window faced a chain link-fence. Beyond the fence was an empty field littered with trash and broken bottles that glinted in the winter sunshine. Lan didn't need the bedroom for himself, but when Sieu An and Johnny came to live with him, they'd have that room. Then Lan would sleep on the sofa.

A table and two plastic chairs mended with electrical tape were crowded into the tiny kitchen. The

42

linoleum was worn through to the backing, and Lan discovered mouse droppings in the drawers. Paint peeled in long strips around the bathtub.

The day he moved in, the apartment had looked pretty bad—much worse than when he had taken a quick look at it and paid the first and last months' rent plus a damage deposit to the woman who reeled off the rules, her cigarette bobbing up and down between her lips. "Better take your bike inside," she warned him, "if you want to find it in the morning."

Bad as it looked, though, the apartment had several advantages. One, he could afford it on what he earned working weekends and a couple of week nights at Red's Diner. Two, it was still in the Roosevelt High School district, and he could ride his bike to school. Three, it wasn't far from Red's Diner; in fact Red's was closer than when he was living at Havilands'. And finally, it was neutral territory for Sieu An—once she came here, surely she'd see how Wayne was ruining her life and Johnny's, too.

He would never forget his first day in the apartment, only two days ago.

After thirteen hours in the kitchen at Red's Diner on New Year's Day, Lan had hauled his bicycle up the outside stairway, flung himself down on the bed, and slept soundly until daylight woke him. Lan had surveyed the apartment with a critical eye, trying to imagine how it would look to Jenny and Rob, and to April, when they saw it for the first time.

"Do you need help moving?" Jenny had asked Lan once she'd finally accepted the fact that he was going through with his plan. "I'll call Rob, and we'll bring your boxes in the truck. I'm sure I can get some of the other kids to help, too."

Lan had begun cleaning, tackling the kitchen first,

to get as much as possible finished before the others came. At eleven o'clock Jenny and Rob arrived. Minutes later Angie and April arrived in Angie's grandfather's car, and then Kurt pulled up in his red Alfa Romeo.

"Nice place," Kurt said, looking around. They were all trying to act enthusiastic for Lan's sake, but he knew better than to believe them.

"It will be when we get through with it," Jenny declared.

Good old bossy Jenny, Lan thought; she was always taking over, always getting things moving. He hoped she had forgiven him for selling Lissa's viola to get money for the apartment. There were times when her bossiness irritated him, but he had to admit that if it hadn't been for Jenny, there probably wouldn't be a hotline.

"Where'd you get the fabulous tan, Kurt?" Angie asked.

"Skiing in Colorado," he said. "It was great. So how've you all been? Lan?"

"New year, new life," Lan said with a smile, wondering if Kurt could understand that. Tall, blond, handsome Kurt, who seemed to have everything.

"Notice anything different about Jenny?" Angie asked Kurt.

Kurt looked Jenny over carefully. "No glasses? You got contacts?"

Jenny grinned happily. "Yep. Santa Claus brought them. Now here's my idea. Lan, if you'd get some paint, I'm sure we can get this place painted today. It wouldn't take long with all of us working. And we could rent a machine and clean the carpets. That would make a huge difference."

Lan originally had thought they'd come, drop off the

boxes, and then leave him to decide where he wanted to put his few things. He wasn't sure how he felt about all the help. And there was the matter of money. But he knew it would be easier to persuade his sister to live there if the place looked decent. "How much paint do you think it would take, Jenny? I can't afford to spend too much."

"We can go to my place first. I think my dad bought some a couple of years ago when he was going to paint the solar room, but he never got around to it and my mother finally hired somebody to do it. I think that paint's still there, and I'm sure he'd let us have it."

"My grandpa's got some leftover paint, too," Angie added. "Maybe not enough for a whole room, though."

"That would be okay, wouldn't it, Lan? If all the walls didn't match exactly?"

"It might start a new trend in decorating," Kurt suggested.

In about five minutes Jenny had devised a plan. She and Lan would drive to her house. Angie was to go home to borrow her grandfather's paint rollers and a stepladder, with Rob and April along to help her. Kurt would pick up the Lundquists' vacuum cleaner, which had a rug shampooer attachment, so they wouldn't have to rent one. Everyone went off in different directions.

Angie returned with not only the painting equipment but with more boxes. "Curtains, sheets, and a bedspread," she explained. "And some dishes. Grandma's always buying new ones. It drives Grandpa crazy." She smiled warmly at Lan and he grinned back shyly. They also brought a tape player and a plate of the brownies her grandmother had just taken out of the oven, plus a gallon of milk from the Circle K.

"If we're going to paint," Rob said, "wouldn't it be

45

better if we got these boxes out of here? Take them back down to the truck until we're finished?"

Lan bit his lip. "Better not," he said. "They'd probably get stolen." He hated to admit that was the kind of neighborhood he had moved into.

"In that case," Kurt said, "let's stash them all in the closets for now."

Five of them had tackled the living room walls and woodwork, while Kurt, who had also brought along a toolbox, worked on the broken furniture. "I didn't think you could fix it if it didn't have at least four cylinders," Angie teased him. He turned out to be a good carpenter, too, though. When the painters moved on to the bedroom, Kurt tackled the carpet in the living room with the steam cleaner.

As they were finishing up, Ilana Feldman and her brother Steven arrived. "I called your house, Jenny," Ilana said. "Your mom told me where you were."

"Who's the giant downstairs, Lan?" Steven asked.

"What giant?"

"If you've seen him, you'd know who we mean," Ilana explained. "This *huge* guy, at least six-six and maybe three hundred pounds, with a shiny bald head. And practically no clothes in this weather."

"No *clothes*?"

"Well, not many. No shirt, anyway—just a little leather vest and jeans. And he didn't even look cold."

"And a dagger as an earring," Steven added. "Don't forget the lethal earring."

"I haven't met my neighbors," Lan explained.

Steven immediately began an inspection, finding places that the painters had missed or spots that had dripped. "One more word out of you, Steven," Jenny threatened, "and I will paint your *face*."

Lan sank down on the sagging sofa and looked

46

around. He could not remember being this tired, even after double shifts at Red's Diner, but the apartment looked a thousand percent better.

"I can't believe we have school tomorrow," Jenny moaned, stretched out flat on the damp but now fairly clean carpet.

"Better believe it, girl," Rob told her unsympathetically.

There was a knock at the door. "Pizza!" someone shouted.

"Pizza?" They all roused from where they had collapsed. "Who read our minds?"

Lan stepped over the fallen bodies of his weary comrades and opened the door. There stood Jack Mertz in his Pizza-on-Wheels jacket and cap, a couple of large, flat boxes in his hands. "I had a call from a Professor R. Haviland, reportedly concerned about malnourished workers at this address, who sends you two pepperoni, green-chile, double-cheese pizzas with his compliments. But I have also been asked to deliver a message to Ms. Jennifer Haviland, to the effect that this is a school night and she is to have her body home by nine o'clock or suffer dire consequences."

"That's my dad," Jenny breathed, looking half pleased and half annoyed.

Lan knew that look well. The quirky humor was one of the things he was going to miss about living at the Havilands. But no one else was paying any attention to Jenny's message. They were too busy devouring pizza.

Now, only forty-eight hours later, was Lan's first session with Adam, and Adam was tense.

"First," Lan instructed, "you must learn to relax. Stop fighting with the instrument. You have a beautiful viola. Make it your friend."

Lan talked quietly, watching as his calming words

took effect on the nervous boy standing in front of him, gripping the precious viola like a weapon. Then Lan picked up Adam's old viola and began to play along with him, going slowly through the warm-up exercises. "Get it right first, feel secure with the notes first," he counseled.

It was painful to watch Adam struggling so hard for what came so easily to Lan. Lan did his best to keep encouraging his pupil, but at the same time not letting up, making Adam really work. He hated to be such a hard taskmaster, but he knew that Mr. Ellis would be even harder.

After a half hour, Lan called for a five-minute break. Adam was sweating. "Please tell me," Lan said, getting them each a glass of water, the only hospitality he could offer, "why is it so important for you to play the viola?"

Adam gulped down the water. "It's really important to my mom that I stay with it. She used to play the violin, and I guess she has it in her mind that I'm going to be a musician. She wanted all of her sons to play something, and I'm the only one who stuck with it. That's the way my folks are—my dad wanted us all to be athletes, but that didn't work out either, except for my brother. Nathaniel was state diving champion, until he went to college. Then, well, I guess he got interested in other things."

"You don't really like it, though, do you?"

"Not really. I mean I do, but it's hard. I thought the new viola would help."

"Maybe it will. Give yourself a little time. When's the next audition?"

"In three weeks," he said. "When the next semester begins."

It's going to take a miracle, Lan thought. *But I'll try.*

PART II

Lessons

Friday, January 5

"**W**e really shouldn't be doing this," Lan protested as April laid out the food on two desks she had pushed together. But they had been doing this on a regular basis since April had discovered a classroom that wasn't locked over lunch period. Getting caught wasn't something April worried about.

"It seems like the only time we can get together, Lan," April said, unwrapping a sandwich. "So I say, make the most of it. If your schedule ever changes so we can spend time at your apartment, this place won't be so important."

When Lan had been living with the Havilands, he had sometimes brought leftovers for lunch or bought lunch in the cafeteria, if he ate at all. But April had decided that the school cafeteria was not the way to go. "Never mind that it's cheap," she announced. "The food is terrible. Worse than terrible. I'll pick up enough for both of us at the supermarket deli."

Lan insisted on paying his share, but he still wasn't sure he liked this idea. It didn't seem right. And that mattered to Lan more than April probably realized.

"Are we ever, ever, *ever* going to be able to spend time together like normal people?" April complained as they ate. "Seems like you work all the time now."

"Seems like it to me, too," Lan admitted. "And now I have another job."

"Another job!" she exploded. "You're already working full weekends and two weeknights at Red's. Then there's the night you work for Jenny's family. Isn't that *enough*, Lan?"

"No, April, it's not," Lan said quietly. "Not when you have to earn enough to live on and take care of other people, too. But this new job is just temporary, and it's only a couple of hours a week. I promised to work with Adam Wolf, the guy who bought my viola. He has to reaudition for Youth Symphony in a few weeks, and he's real nervous about it. He asked if I'd kind of coach him until then, and he offered me good money. So I said I'd do it. I had to."

April fumed. "I would not have believed I'd get involved with a boy who was never able to spend any time with me. Do you realize that the only times we're together are forty minutes at lunch and a little while after school in the hotline room? It's just not fair! I thought once you got your own apartment, we'd be together a lot more."

"I'm sorry, April." He really *was* sorry and he racked his brain for a way to make it up to her. "How about if we do something tonight? I'm Kristen's partner on the hotline until six, but after that I'm free. I'll make dinner for you at my apartment, if you'd like to come over."

April's face brightened immediately. "I'd love to! I already know which buses to take to get there. I checked the schedule. What time should I come over?"

"I'll pick you up at your place at seven-thirty." Lan didn't want to tell her he was afraid for her to come into his neighborhood by herself.

"*Another* call about drugs? I can't believe it!" Jenny said. "It's like an epidemic or something. What was it this time, Kurt?"

Lan set his chair close by the door to the inner office, in case Kristen Hallett needed him while she was on duty. There was no official hotline meeting today, just the usual hanging out for a while before everyone split for the weekend.

"It was from a guy who calls himself Ninja," Kurt said. "He called near the end of my shift yesterday. Says he's worried about his brother, who's a dealer."

"Ninja?" April repeated. "That's a weird name. Why do you suppose he picked that name?"

"I have no idea," Kurt said. "And it doesn't seem to have any connection with his story." Kurt outlined the call for the hotliners.

"It sounds kind of like Star's situation," Jenny said, shaking her head sadly. "Poor kids!"

"Did you get any calls about Karen or Joseph?" Rob asked.

"One," Kurt said. "From a girl who said she knew for the past month that Joseph was into drugs, and she hadn't done anything about it. She was feeling pretty guilty. Basically she just wanted to talk to somebody about how bad she felt. All I did was listen."

"I've been thinking," Jason Aragon said slowly. "I've been thinking that maybe the hotline should launch an anti-drug campaign."

Jason was one of the newer members of the hotline, and Lan was impressed with the way he had handled himself so far, the kinds of things he said. All Lan

53

knew about Jason before he came on the hotline was that he was a talented artist and did a regular cartoon strip for the *B&G* called "Short Stop." Jason himself was short—at least three inches shorter than Lan's five feet seven—and looked much younger than seventeen, but he seemed to handle all that fairly well. The characters in Jason's drawings were always tiny figures taking on gigantic opponents, and the results were very funny.

"Say more, Jason," Jenny urged him. "Why? How?"

"*Why* is simple," Jason explained. "Because so many kids are involved with drugs, or at least *affected* by drugs. Like Star and Ninja. So I was thinking we could get some training to go around and make presentations in classes. I could put together a cartoon slide show, and we could put posters up around campus." He turned to Jenny. "Run a big spread in the *B&G*. Get everybody to wear an anti-drug badge. Have people tie ribbons to their cars. You know, just keep hammering on the idea until everybody is super-aware of it."

"Sounds like a lot of work, Jason," Rob said. "We'd be taking on another big project, besides the hotline."

"Too much, Jason," Steven agreed. "We have numbers we refer people to who have problems with drugs, like the Narcotics Anonymous number."

"I agree with Jason," Nikki said. "The hotline is a high-visibility group. Everybody in the school knows about it. Everybody knows we do good work. That makes us the perfect group to go public with the message. So why not do what Jason says? Maybe not all of it, but at least some."

"We shouldn't spread ourselves too thin," Michelle said. "That's what I think."

Lan listened to the debate swirling around him, this

one for, this one against, unsure how he really felt. On the one hand, Jason was right—they were in an ideal position to launch a spectacular anti-drug campaign at Roosevelt. But on the other hand, Steven had a point. The hotline ought to get all their efforts. Lan didn't agree with Nikki, though, that everybody knew about Ears. Probably there were still kids around school who hadn't heard about the hotline, or were afraid to call, or didn't think it applied to them. Maybe that's where their energies should go.

"What do you think, Lan?"

Lan considered carefully before he spoke. "The one thing I know for sure," he said, "is that I'm dead set against drugs, any kind of drugs, and whatever will help to get rid of them, I'm in favor of."

As he was talking, Lan noticed Kurt leaning forward intently. "I'd just like to say," Kurt began, "that whether we decide to run an anti-drug campaign or stick with being the hotline and only the hotline, there's something I believe we need to do as a group. That is," he said slowly, as though he was searching for exactly the right words, "I think all of us on the hotline should sign a pledge to be drug-free. I mean *totally* drug-free. Not only promise that we're not going to smoke dope or crack or shoot heroin or whatever. That's obvious. But pledge not to drink anything alcoholic. We're all underage for drinking in this state anyway, but I know that at least some of us manage to get beer and stuff when we want it." *Including me*, Kurt thought wryly.

"What about cigarettes?" Rob asked.

Kurt nodded. "No cigarettes, either. Smoking's not illegal, but it's an addiction that could ruin our bodies. I think if we're going to be on the hotline and trying to help kids with problems, then we need to be a hundred-percent clean ourselves. Maybe we could all sign a big poster and put it up on the main bulletin board and get other kids to add their names."

"Not a bad idea," Jenny said. "In fact, it's terrific. It makes it absolutely clear where we stand. I can't imagine anybody who'd object."

"I do," Michelle Piper said, her voice sharp-edged. "I think it's a really stupid idea and totally unnecessary. Everybody *knows* this group and what we stand for. So why make a big deal about this pledge?"

Lan looked at Michelle in surprise. Like him, Michelle never had much to say in the group, so her outburst was kind of surprising. On the other hand, he knew that Michelle was probably under a lot of stress, with her parents splitting up after that awful public scandal. And she was the one person in the group who had actually known Karen and Joseph.

"Gee, Michelle," Jenny said, "why do you think it's such a bad idea?"

"I just do. And I really don't want to talk about it," Michelle muttered.

But then Lan's attention was caught by the ringing of the phone. Kristen answered and motioned him to come inside. Lan picked up his chair and moved, closing the door behind him.

"Ninja," Kristen scrawled on a piece of paper and shoved it toward him.

Kurt held the door as Michelle slid into the passenger seat of his Alfa. "Any place you'd like to go?" he asked.

"Home," she whispered.

Kurt drove quickly out of the parking lot. He was still thinking about the pledge he'd suggested. He'd been thinking about it since long before today, as a matter of fact. He was willing to give up his occasional beer, especially if it was going to set the right example for others. He didn't think he could reach his mother with her ever-full wineglass, but maybe it could work for his fifteen-year-old sister, Dana.

Now, as he drove toward Mountain Shadow Estates, where he and Michelle both lived, he thought about their relationship. He was a little surprised that he and Michelle still managed to be friends, in spite of the blow-up a couple of months ago. It had been a painful time for everybody. His own parents were still together, more or less the way they had always been, but Michelle's were going through what she called a "trial separation."

Kurt truly did care about Michelle, a beautiful, sexy girl who had long attracted him. And he felt sorry for all the bad things that had happened to her. He knew from his own experience that feuding parents could be nerve-wracking. Having them split up must be pretty awful, too.

"You want to talk?" he asked, turning in at the massive gates that flanked the entrance to Mountain Shadows.

She nodded.

"I guess the whole business with Karen and Joseph hit you pretty hard," he ventured.

She shrugged.

Not much of a conversation, Kurt thought. He debated whether to take her to her own home and risk running into her mother, which he dreaded, or take her to his house. He decided his house was less of a risk. He was pretty sure his mother was either not at home or shut up in her bedroom with a glass of wine. And his father was either at his car dealership or down at City Hall.

But he hadn't figured on Dana being there. His sister spent hardly any time at home, breezing in and out when it suited her to change one ratty set of clothes for another. Kurt figured she was staying mostly with her boyfriend Greg Hurd, Hurd the Nerd, or with a girlfriend who had her own apartment near the university. The thought of the kind of things Dana might be getting into make him shiver.

"Well hel-*lo*," Dana greeted them. "Fancy seeing you here, Michelle. What have you been doing? Jeez, you look like hell."

"Dana!" Kurt protested.

"Well, it's true! You mean you haven't noticed Michelle looks like a skeleton? How much weight have you lost, Michelle?"

"About twenty-five pounds, that's all," Michelle murmured, looking wretched.

"Well, I think you better put some of it back on. You anorexic or something?"

Kurt grabbed Dana's arm and started to yank her back toward her room. "Shut *up*, brat!" Kurt warned her.

"No, I'm not anorexic, Dana," Michelle said angrily. Then suddenly her anger turned to tears. She covered her face with her hands. "I just tried to lose some weight, because the modeling school I'm going to said I was too fat."

"I thought they told you twenty pounds," Kurt said, releasing his hold on Dana. Suddenly he noticed the dark circles around her eyes. "So why have you lost twenty-five?"

"I lost the extra five just for good measure. But that's all. I'm not going to lose any more."

"How about a milk shake?" Dana said. "A piece of chocolate cake?" Dana stared at her. "You know some-

58

thing, Michelle? I've always thought you were so beautiful. I always wanted to look like you! But you've gotten so skinny. . . . Did you get hooked on diet pills, Michelle? Are you a speed freak?"

"Dana!" Kurt gasped.

Michelle began screaming. "No!" she shrieked. "I am not a speed freak! I do not have a drug problem, *do you hear me?*"

Oh my God, Kurt thought, putting his arms around the hysterical Michelle to shield her from his sister. "Dana," he said evenly, "I want you to leave this room right now. *Do I make myself clear?*"

For once Dana backed off without an argument. The swinging door slapped shut as she left the kitchen.

In his arms, Michelle was completely still. "I'm sorry," Kurt began. "Michelle, I'm really sorry about that. Dana is such a brat—"

Michelle moved out of his awkward embrace. "It's all right, Kurt," she said calmly, and when he continued to apologize she placed a cool finger on his lips. "Just forget it, okay?" she said. "You're right, though. She *is* a brat. That mouth could get her into a lot of trouble some day." Michelle picked up her purse and books and headed for the back door. "I've got to be going," she said, almost cheerily.

"Wait, I'll drive you," Kurt said.

"No, don't bother. I live right around the corner, remember?" And she was gone.

Lan paced, pausing now and then to look out the window of his apartment.

Earlier in the day Lan had thought he'd had the whole evening planned. He would come home after the hotline shift with Kristen, drop off his books, and head straight to the grocery story to buy dinner ingredients. That would give him barely enough time to shower and catch the bus to get to April's by seven-thirty.

He should have known better than to try to nail down the unpredictable April. She had intercepted him on the way to the hotline room and said, "Forget Plan A. We're doing Plan B—that is, don't come to my place. I'll get to your apartment on my own. And don't do any cooking before I get there."

"April, this is not a good idea," he had protested.

"Oh, Lan! Come on! I want to bring you a surprise, and it won't be a surprise if you come for me."

That was the sort of thing she was always doing. Sometimes it was fun, but it also made him feel a little off-balance. Lan preferred things to be laid out, neat and organized, and predictable.

So he had agreed, and now he regretted it. She was already fifteen minutes late. Finally he grabbed his jacket and rushed down the steps. He caught a glimpse of the bald giant with bulging biceps unlocking the door to the apartment directly below his. The giant nodded once to Lan, and Lan nodded in reply.

He took a shortcut around the end of the building and trotted the four blocks to Central Avenue. There was no sign of April.

He almost missed the bus coming from the direction opposite the one he was expecting, almost didn't see the dark-haired girl who stepped off and was hurrying down the street away from him. *April!* "What were you doing on *that* bus?" he demanded when he caught up with her.

"You'll find out," she said mysteriously, giving him her free hand. She kept a grocery bag firmly clutched in the other arm.

60

"Here, let me carry that."

"Nope. I told you, it's a surprise."

Lan shook his head; April and her surprises. They hurried to the apartment without talking, their chins tucked into their chests and tears running down their cheeks from the cold.

She set the bag on the little kitchen table and looked around the apartment. "Lan, it's wonderful," April said, her pretty face lit up with a smile.

Lan smiled back. "That's not exactly how I'd describe it. But thank you. At least it's mine." He knew she expected him to kiss her, and he was happy to do so. "Your nose is cold."

"It's warming up fast," she sighed and leaned against him. "Okay," she said, pulling away. "Time to celebrate."

Lan eyed the grocery bag suspiciously. "Please, no champagne!" he said.

"No, I'm signing Jason's pledge—no more champagne. But now I have another problem," she said earnestly.

"What's that?"

"I'm addicted to *you*."

Lan hugged her, feeling both pleased and embarrassed. Part of April's charm was her saying outrageous things. "What did you bring? Something from Take-A-Taco?" He hoped not; Lan had gone with her once to the Mexican fast-food place where she worked a few hours a week. He thought the food was awful, but he didn't want to tell her how bad.

"You're not even close," she said, unpacking the shopping bag. "I know how you feel about Take-A-Taco—you can't fool me. This is a treat for you, so I got something I was sure you'd like. Welcome to your new home."

61

Lan stared at the small containers she was lining up on the counter, not believing what he saw. "What is it?"

"I went to the Saigon Café and got some Vietnamese take-out," she answered with a grin. "I feel like I've been riding buses all over town. That's why I was on the bus going the opposite direction."

Lan was amazed and touched by her thoughtfulness. He was also curious. He hadn't dared go to the restaurant, although he had called Sieu An from Red's a couple of times, to ask how she was. Her reply was always the same: "We're fine." And he had to believe her, although he doubted that she was telling the truth.

"Did you see my sister?" Lan asked.

"Yes. I told her I was your friend. She said to say hello."

"Did she look all right? Did you see Johnny? What about Wayne?"

"Your sister looked good. She seemed happy to know I was bringing this stuff back here to you. Wayne was back in the kitchen so I didn't see him, but I did see your adorable nephew. Johnny looked fine, except for his broken arm."

"Broken arm! How did he get a broken arm? Did they tell you?"

April shrugged and began searching for plates and utensils. "I asked him, and he just said, 'I had a accident.' He didn't say what kind of accident, and Sieu An didn't say either."

Lan sat down on the sofa and propped his head in his hands. All kinds of terrible images swirled in his mind. "Something bad must have happened to him," he said. Could Wayne have hurt his own son so badly? Remembering Wayne's violent temper, Lan jumped up and started pacing. "I have to get them away from there. It's not safe for them to live with him!"

April tried to calm him down. "Look, you don't know that's what happened to Johnny. Maybe he fell off the swings at kindergarten or something. You don't know that Wayne did anything to him. There's not much you can do. You can't just rush in there and grab Johnny, you know." She sat down next to Lan on the couch and stroked his arm. "I see how much it bothers you. I know you care a lot about them. But you have to slow down a little."

He looked at her. April was a nice girl, he was deeply fond of her, and she seemed to understand him very well, but there were some things she *didn't* understand—mostly that he was responsible for his family. This weekend he would go to the Saigon Café and find out for himself.

Then he forced himself to remember that this was April's celebration. She had gone to a lot of trouble to please him, and the least he could do was act as though he enjoyed it. "Thank you for doing all this, April," he said. "It's terrific."

"You're welcome," she replied, poking into one of the containers of food. "Now tell me what all this stuff *is*."

Lan insisted on cleaning up the dishes as soon as they were finished. He knew that April would have left the dirty dishes in the sink at her home, or maybe even left them on the table, but at his place, things would be washed and put away right away.

"I almost forgot—did you and Kristen get any interesting calls?" April asked, drying as Lan washed.

"Yes—Kristen took another call from Ninja. It's hard to tell what's really going on there. He calls, he's

63

upset, he needs to talk about his brother, and then he backs off and says everything is really okay."

"I don't believe that, do you? That everything is okay?"

"No." Lan wiped off the kitchen table and set up his chess pieces. "But at least we're there for him to talk to."

They had played only a couple of times since he started teaching her at Thanksgiving, and Lan was pretty sure five-year-old Johnny could beat her without much trouble. She had been eager to learn, but tonight she couldn't seem to concentrate, and neither could Lan. All Lan could think about was Johnny and his broken arm.

"I'm thinking of quitting my job, I hate it so much," April told him, absent-mindedly moving her queen into a vulnerable position, "but I have to repay all that money."

"All what money?"

"From the phone bill I ran up. I thought I told you about that. I got on one of those chat lines and talked about a thousand dollars' worth of minutes. It adds up so fast! So I have to pay my dad back for all of that, before I get to keep any for myself. I'll be an old lady before I get it paid off!"

They gave up on chess and ended up making out. Lan was relieved that they had agreed on limits, and April didn't suggest that they make love. Lan didn't feel ready for that big step in their relationship. His body was ready—that was an embarrassing problem—but his head wasn't. After an evening of kissing and cuddling, it was hard to leave the warm apartment and wait, shivering, on a windy street corner for the bus that ran only every half hour.

As they walked from the bus stop to her apartment

building, Lan decided to bring up a subject that had been on his mind for a couple of weeks. "I think I ought to meet your father, April, if we're going to spend a lot of time together," Lan said. "So he knows you're with someone who can be trusted."

"Not a good idea," April said, snuggling against him.

"He knows we're going out together, doesn't he?"

"He knows I have a boyfriend who is brilliant, handsome, and a real gentleman. But if he met you, it might cause problems."

"What kind of problems?" Lan asked.

"My dad was in the war in Vietnam. He . . . he had some bad experiences there. He got addicted to heroin. He managed to kick it, finally, but it really messed up his life." She looked tearful, and Lan was afraid she might cry. "If anything reminds him of the war, he gets real upset. That's all. It's not *you*; it's his own memories. And I don't want to do anything that makes it bad for him."

"Then out of respect for your father maybe we should not be together," Lan said. That's how it would have been in his own country, Lan knew: respect for one's parents, respect for one's elders.

"No," she said. "I love my dad and I feel bad about what he went through, but I can't let it rule *my* life. You didn't have anything to do with that war, Lan. It's not your fault. But it's just not a good idea for you to meet him."

"What happens if he finds out?"

She shrugged. "I'll deal with that when the time comes. Don't worry about it."

But of course he did worry, all the way back to his apartment in the freezing cold.

Saturday, January 6

Angie swept up the floor of the beauty salon after her mother finished the haircut and hurried to answer the ringing phone. "Le Salon de Gilbert," she said.

"Angie?" said a familiar voice. "It's Connie, your wicked stepmother. I'm calling to see if you're free for lunch today."

Her father's new wife was a neat lady, Angie thought, and it sounded like fun to go somewhere with her. "Great," Angie said, "I can leave anytime after one."

They drove to a small, sunny restaurant and ordered soup and salad. "The boys are with their father this weekend," Connie explained with a warm smile, "and I thought we could spend some time together and do a little catch-up. So tell me—how's your job? You enjoy working at the salon?"

"Not really," Angie admitted, nibbling a cracker. "It might not be so bad if the owner wasn't such a jerk. He makes us call him *jeel-BEAR*, like he's really fooling people into thinking he's French. I'd love to get a job somewhere else, but nothing's come up. And it's better than a place like Take-A-Taco, where one of my friends works."

"Keep your eyes open," Connie advised. "You'll find something you like." The waitress arrived with their lunches, and as soon as she had gone, Connie asked, "What about Marcos?"

"I broke up with him a long time ago. Around Thanksgiving. I thought you knew that."

Connie nodded. "I wasn't sure you'd *stay* broken up. Sometimes it takes people a long time."

"Not me," Angie said. "Once I decided to do it, I did it, and that was that."

"Good for you!" Connie said. "And the hotline? Are you still involved in it?"

"Oh, yes!" Angie told her stepmother about the kinds of calls they had been getting, and about Lan and his new apartment.

"Now I have something to tell *you*," Connie said. "I'm becoming an actress, and I want you to come and see me. I'm in a play we're putting on at the Hispanic Heritage Center."

"Connie! That's so exciting! I didn't know you were doing anything like that."

"It's a bilingual theater group, and I got involved because I'm trying to improve my Spanish. You know, I was never into this kind of thing before, but now I love it."

"I want to improve my Spanish, too," Angie said. "My teacher, Señora Gonzales, says I have a good ear but I need to concentrate more on grammar."

"The Center isn't only about speaking grammatically correct Spanish, Angie. It's about who you are, your background, your history. I bet you'd like it there, too."

"Well, maybe so. My mom always says we should try to be good Americans and forget all this ethnic stuff."

Connie paused to think about that. "Look, I'm not going to contradict your mother. But I think part of being a good American is understanding your roots. And your roots are strong and rich, Angie. You should be proud of your heritage. Why don't you come to the play next weekend?" she suggested. "We're going to have a fiesta afterward—you know, a mariachi band, lots of food. It's going to be a lot of fun, Angie. Bring a friend if you like."

"I'll be there for sure," Angie said, wondering who she could take. Then she thought of Jack Mertz.

Moving to his own apartment had its advantages, Lan decided, but there was also the down side. He needed a new alarm clock, for one thing; his old one wasn't reliable, and he had barely made it to work on time this morning. He had to be at Red's at six, in order to have the first batch of muffins ready by seven when the diner opened. Red's specialty was twelve kinds of muffins, and Lan had somehow become the muffin master.

Lan had hauled his bike down the stairs from the balcony to the parking lot. The building was silent then, long before sunrise, although it had been anything but silent only a couple of hours before. By the time he had taken April home and gotten back to his apartment, it was almost one o'clock in the morning. Instead of going to sleep, he lay there thinking of Sieu An, kept away by the monotonous thud of heavy metal music and occasional loud voices in the downstairs apartment. Lan had mashed his flimsy pillow over his ears to try to block out the noise, but it didn't work. During the night he went to the bathroom and discovered that he could hear voices quite distinctly from down below, almost make out what they were saying, as though the pipes carried the sound directly from that apartment into his.

Later on, still unable to sleep, he had gotten up and peered through the slats of the blinds into the parking lot. He saw the bald giant carrying a limp body in his arms; somebody either completely drunk or drugged out, Lan thought with disgust. A small, thin man in a dark business suit and a third man in a ski jacket opened the rear door of a blue panel truck. The giant shoved the limp body inside and drove away in the truck. Seconds later Lan saw the small man climb into a black sedan and glide silently away. Then the man in the ski jacket left in an expensive sports car.

Lan went back to bed. Finally, at three A.M., the building was silent. At last he could sleep.

During his first break that morning he called the Saigon Café; luckily his sister picked up the phone on the first ring.

"I want to see you, Sieu An," he said. "It's important. Tell me when you think you're going to be alone, and I'll be there." Lan was scheduled to work all weekend, but he was pretty sure he could get a couple of hours off and make them up later.

"Tomorrow," she murmured. "Three o'clock."

Lan went back to work. The lunch rush was at its peak when Brenda, the waitress, delivered a message. "There's a kid with a big violin out there wants to see you. Said his name is Adam."

"Tell him I'll be out in a few minutes." Maybe he's brought the money, Lan thought, hurrying to fill some orders before he went out to the main dining room; that would be good.

"Hi, Adam," Lan said, wiping his hands on his

69

apron. "This is a real busy time, so I've only got about three minutes. How's it going?"

Adam shrugged. "Not too well. Ellis was on my case twice this morning. And he stopped me on the way out and asked if I was getting ready for the reauditions. I told him you're coaching me. He said to tell you how much he misses having you in the Youth Symphony. I do too, Lan! I sure hope I can pull this off."

"You can. You just have to work at it." Lan watched Adam fidget nervously and thought to himself, *he didn't bring the money; I can see that*.

"Look, the reason I'm here is to ask if you could possibly spend some more time with me. I know, I have to do it myself, but it really helps a lot when you go over the stuff with me. It *feels* better. And it makes me practice more. I know I don't have any right to ask this, Lan, but if there's anything I can do for you, any favor besides the money I'll pay you, just say the word, and I'll do it."

The idea came to Lan out of nowhere, like a lightning flash. He didn't even stop to think about it. "There *is* something," he said. "Would you teach me to drive? I must be the only student at Roosevelt who can't."

"You mean the motorcycle?"

"No—that car you sometimes drive. The Jeep."

Adam grinned at him, relief spreading across his face. "You've got a deal," he said. "Now all we have to do is figure out *when*." They shook hands, and Lan stood up to go back to the kitchen. But Adam didn't move. "There's one other thing, Lan, if you've got just a second."

Lan nodded, waiting, hoping at least it wasn't *bad* news about the money.

"This hotline you've been telling me about? Well—

70

I've been wondering . . . who the people are, you know? And how they got picked and trained. And do they really know what they're talking about? I mean, so I could get one started at Academy. You'd be surprised how screwed up a lot of my classmates are. A lot of people think that because we go to a private school that everybody has tons of money and no problems, like being rich guarantees you've got a perfect life. That's not true at all, Lan, and not everybody there is even that rich."

Lan stepped back, a little surprised at this outburst. Adam had always seemed pretty laid back to Lan, but tonight he was different.

"I really don't have time to talk about the hotline now," Lan said. "But I can tell you that our hotliners are good. We've been trained to listen, that's the main thing. Next time I see you we'll talk about it, okay?"

Catching up on orders back in the kitchen, Lan thought about the driving lessons. This new development cheered him up, although it meant more work on an already impossibly tight schedule. He could hardly wait to tell his sister.

"I want to apologize, Kurt," Michelle said. "I feel bad about the way I came so totally unglued with you and Dana."

"It's okay. I understand. I figured the . . . the deaths had gotten to you, and you kind of lost it."

But Kurt wasn't sure he really did understand, because there seemed to be more to it than that. Dana was convinced that Michelle was hooked on diet pills, speed, and that it had started when she decided to lose weight for the stupid modeling school. The more Michelle told him about that place, the surer he was that she ought to get away from it.

71

To try to make peace with her after the blow-up, he had invited her to go out to dinner and maybe a movie. Normally she used to love to go out and eat, but now she just picked at the food on her plate and finally pushed it aside, almost untouched. He wondered if he could say something to her about it, get her talking about what was happening in her life. But she seemed so jumpy and tense that he was afraid to bring up anything serious. If she wanted to talk about Karen and Joseph, she'd have to mention it herself.

"I'm going to come right out and ask you, Kurt," she said finally, brushing aside a lock of auburn hair, "since it doesn't look like you're going to ask me. Who are you taking to the Mayor's Ball? I guess that's a question everybody wants to ask the mayor's son."

Warning bells went off. He knew she wanted him to ask her, but he had made up his mind that it was not possible, not after all the stories in the press about their parents' affair, even though all that was past. Surely Michelle would understand that it was impossible.

Besides which, his father had suggested strongly, in that way he had, that Kurt's duty was to escort Rachel Steinway. Known around school as Steinway Grand for her excess poundage, Rachel was the daughter of a heavy-hitter in his father's campaign for mayor, and it was understood that there were times when personal preference didn't count as much as keeping his father happy. In this case that meant keeping Mr. Steinway's daughter happy.

"Look, Michelle," he began as diplomatically as he knew how, "it would be great to go to the ball with you. But given all the bad publicity about our families, I think it's out of the question. And my father has prac-

72

tically ordered me to take Rachel." Michelle's smile abruptly faded.

"I thought the campaign was over," she complained. "I thought now you could go back to doing what you want."

"Not quite."

Kurt was actually surprised Michelle would even ask in the first place, much less push the issue. After the scandal surrounding their parents, the idea of Kurt and Michelle pairing up at the Mayor's Ball was pretty questionable. Even more surprising was the way Michelle seemed to be taking it.

She looked as if she was on the verge of tears. He didn't remember her being like this before, ready to cry or throw a tantrum whenever she didn't get what she wanted. Quiet, reserved, ladylike, Michelle didn't seem like herself at all any more. Kurt hardly knew this new Michelle, and he didn't like her much.

It had to be the drugs, Kurt thought; the diet pills. Dana was right. They'd changed her whole personality. He felt he had to do something to help her get back her old self, before that self was lost forever.

"Michelle, listen," he said, reaching out to take her hand. "I want to talk to you about something. Something very serious."

She turned her luminous brown eyes on him, and he noticed again the dark circles that at first he had thought were makeup. "What?" she asked petulantly.

He decided to go for it. "Those diet pills. The amphetamines. Whatever speedy thing it is you're doing to yourself that's making a wreck of you."

Instantly her expression changed, her eyes narrowed, her mouth hardened. "You and that bitch of a

73

sister of yours," she said in a cruel, angry voice. "Why don't you both mind your own business?"

Kurt didn't back down. "This is my business," he said. "You're my friend. I want to help you."

"*Help* me!" she fairly shouted, and Kurt realized, too late, that he should never have brought up the subject in a public place. He had hoped that being in front of people would keep her calm, but it didn't. "Why don't you worry about your own problems, *asshole*!"

Michelle had been clutching the stem of her water goblet; now she abruptly slammed the goblet back on the table. There was a crack, the sound of glass breaking, as the fragile stem snapped and water drenched the table. With an inarticulate cry, she jumped up suddenly from the table and rushed for the exit.

Kurt quickly dug in his pocket, dropped a handful of bills on the table to pay for the meal, and ran after her.

He found her sobbing against his car. "Come on," he said as gently as he could. "I'll take you home. Get in."

Michelle continued to weep softly as Kurt drove, finally calming down after a few minutes while Kurt remained silent. "It's the tension," she said after a while. "You don't know what it's like. My mom and all."

"It's not your mom," he said doggedly. "It's drugs, Michelle."

"*It . . . is . . . not . . . drugs*," she said through clenched teeth.

Kurt decided to drop it for now. But how was he ever going to help her when she kept denying the problem?

Sunday, January 7

"Look at this, look at this!" Jenny crowed, waving the feature section of the Sunday *Tribune* under her father's nose. "Doesn't it look *great*?"

Mr. Haviland adjusted his glasses and inspected the full page of photographs and text. The headline read CITY YOUTH SYMPHONY HITS HIGH NOTE, with the by-line, "Text by Jennifer Haviland. Photos by Robert Saylor." Ms. Moore-Haviland came to read over her husband's shoulder while Jenny marveled at the piece again.

"I wonder if Rob's seen it yet. Maybe it's not too early to call him."

"Well, why don't you?" her mother said. "Invite him over for brunch, if you want to."

Jenny danced off to her father's study to make the call. "I didn't wake you up, did I?" she asked when she heard Rob's groggy voice.

"No. No, you didn't wake me up, Jenny." He yawned luxuriously.

"I guess I did. It sounds like you're still asleep. Have you seen the paper yet?"

"Huh-uh." Suddenly he sounded fully alert. "Is our article in? How does it look?"

"Terrific! We even got a big by-line. I can't wait for you to see it. Come over for brunch and we'll celebrate."

"Sounds good. Then I have to take my parents to the airport. They're leaving at three o'clock."

"It's my dad's turn to cook, and it may take a while for him to actually *produce* anything. But come as soon as you can."

Jenny rushed back to her room and changed out of her gray sweats with the holes in the knees to jeans and a big sweater. Then, as she always did when she was taking pains to look especially nice, she brushed her brown hair back from her face and fastened it with the silver and turquoise hair clip Lissa had given her the afternoon before she died. Every time Jenny wore it, she thought of Lissa. The memory made her sad, but it was no longer the searing pain it had been during those first awful weeks. *So much has happened since then,* Jenny thought. *If only Lissa were still here to share it all with.*

Determinedly she brushed away the cobwebby feelings of sadness and went out to set the table and see what she could do to help her father. A month ago it wouldn't have been a problem, Jenny recalled. Lan would have fixed something delicious. She realized how much she missed having Lan around—not just the superb meals he produced, but his calm, sensible company. She never would have expected to feel that way.

"People come into our lives and then they leave again," her mother had said at dinner the other night when Jenny had wondered aloud for the umpteenth time why Lan had decided to move to his own apartment. "That's the way life is, Jenny. All we can do is be grateful for those times we have with people we care about, and then let them go when we must. In fact, Jenny," Ms. Moore-Haviland continued, "your father and I must get used to the idea that one of these days you'll be going off to college, the beginning of a life of your own."

College: the idea excited Jenny. She planned to major in journalism, and lately she had been daydreaming about how neat it would be if someday she and Rob could work as a team—Rob taking the pictures, Jenny doing the writing. Maybe they'd even do a book together or make a film. *Maybe get married and travel around the world together,* Jenny thought. *It would be so great!*

Rob arrived as she was arranging place mats and napkins on the kitchen table. Her father solved the brunch problem by picking up fruit salad and croissants at a gourmet grocery that had just opened in their neighborhood. "In the nick of time," her mother had said. "We'll certainly be their favorite customers, now that Lan has gone."

As soon as they had finished eating, Jenny and Rob went over every inch of their photo essay about the Youth Symphony. Jenny was pleased to see that the editor had changed hardly anything in her article, and Rob was pleased that his photographs had reproduced well.

"Maybe we ought to try another article for the *Trib,*" Rob said.

Jenny looked at Rob affectionately. "I've been making a list of ideas," she said. They really were a team. Then her attention returned to the article. "That's a wonderful shot of Lan. He's going to love that picture. He looks like a professional violist, doesn't he? Like somebody you'd see at Carnegie Hall. Could you make a print for him? It would be a nice surprise."

"One for April, too," Rob said. "But she'll probably want it poster size."

"And there's Adam Wolf," Jenny said.

"You know, your tone of voice actually changes when you talk about him. What is it about Adam Wolf that bothers you so much? Just because he bought Lan's viola?"

"I don't know," she admitted. "Just a weird feeling, that's all."

Time flew by, as it always did when she was with Rob. Suddenly he glanced at his watch and jumped to his feet. "Gotta go. They can't stand being late for planes." He planted a loud kiss on her cheek and went looking for her parents to thank them. "I'll call you later," he promised as he trotted down the walk toward his purple VW.

Jenny watched him drive away, and humming to herself, went back to read the newspaper article one more time.

After he had finished his shift at Red's, Lan chained his bike to a pole down the street from the Saigon Café and circled around to make sure Wayne wasn't there. His brother-in-law's banged-up station wagon was gone from its parking place in the alley. The restaurant was dark and a CLOSED sign hung in the window. Lan tapped on the glass door, and a moment later the lock clicked.

"Come in," his sister said. He slipped past her and she locked the door behind him. "I have made some tea," she said with her sweet, sad smile. He sat down at a table and looked around while he waited for her to bring a pot and two cups from the kitchen. There had been some changes at the café: more tables had been added, there was fresh paint, and new curtains hung at the big front window. Lan was pleasantly surprised to see it look so good.

"How are you?" he asked quietly, looking her over carefully.

"Fine," she said, the smile fixed in place. "And you?"

"I'm fine, too. Where's Johnny?"

"With his father. Wayne took him to a movie."

"I wish I could see him."

She nodded. "Johnny misses you. We both do."

Lan had planned to tell her he wanted her to come and live with him, but he sensed that it wouldn't work to do it that way. Not yet. He'd have to take it one step at a time. "Sieu An, I got an apartment. It's big, and pretty nice, too. I want you to come and see it. Here's the address." He laid a piece of paper on the table in front of her. She looked at it carefully, folded it, and put it in the pocket of her skirt. "When can you come?" he pressed.

She shrugged. "It's very hard. We have long hours here. You remember. It's hard for me to get away. And I have no transportation, unless Wayne drives me."

"Taxi," Lan said. "I'll pay for it." It would be expensive, but he'd do it. It was possible to go by bus, but it was a long ride that would involve a couple of changes; he knew she didn't have that much time. And he knew she could not ask Wayne for money for a taxi.

She thought it over. "Next Sunday I will come."

"Can you bring Johnny?"

"I will try."

That gave him a week to get ready. And to think of a way to convince her.

79

Monday, January 8

"**I** know it sounds complicated, April," Lan said. "Adam's picking me up after school and taking me to his house. We're going to practice, I'm supposed to have dinner there, and then he's driving me to Red's. This is only going to last for a few more weeks," he said, "I promise."

"Your schedule is impossible already, Lan," April said with a sigh and squeezed his hand. "But I've got a surprise for you. I might as well tell you now."

"What is it?"

"Are you ready for this?" she asked with a huge grin. "I quit my job at Take-A-Taco."

"You did? But I thought you had to stay there at least until you got that phone bill paid off."

"I don't have to work *there*. I just have to work *somewhere*. So I got a new job. Guess where!"

"I give up. Where?"

"Red's Diner."

"*Red's*? You got a job at Red's?" He was stunned. Why did she go and do that? As if he didn't know.

"Yep," she said, obviously pleased with herself and

her surprise. "I start this weekend. I'm working Saturday and Sunday as a waitress, and more if they need me. Brenda's going to train me. She says the tips are pretty good."

"I see." That's all he trusted himself to say. He wasn't at all sure how he felt about having April work the same place he did. "When were you there? I didn't see you."

"I did it while you were out. Sunday afternoon."

Sunday afternoon. When he was with Sieu An. "I was visiting my sister," he explained.

"How did it go, Lan?" Her smile faded and she looked concerned, twisting a finger in her dark curls.

"All right." The bell rang, and they collected their trash and headed for the door of their private lunchroom. "She's coming to visit next weekend. I want her and Johnny to move into the apartment with me."

"But what about Wayne? He's not going to let her do that, is he?"

"He can't force her to stay."

"But you don't know what *she* wants to do, Lan. After all, she's married to Wayne, and they have Johnny."

"She will want to come and live with me," he said stubbornly. "I'm sure of that."

They hurried through the crowded hallway toward their afternoon class. "I know you're worried about her, Lan," April said sympathetically. "I would be too. But it's her choice, and if she wants to stay with him, you really can't do anything about it."

Lan looked at her. "I don't think you understand," he said.

"I understand a *lot*," she said. Then she did what he was always afraid she was going to do—threw her arms around his neck and kissed him good-bye, right in front of the door to his computer class.

"In the interests of my guilt complex, Angie, please let me drive you home," Jack insisted. "Otherwise you'll freeze to death or catch a cold, and it will be all my fault."

Angie laughed. "I wouldn't want you to feel guilty," she said. "But you know, you can't catch a cold just from *being* cold."

"No? What do you catch a cold from, then?" Jack opened the door of his van and Angie climbed in.

"Viruses. There are hundreds of them. I learned that in health."

"Oh ho. Did you know that the best virus-fighter in the world is hot chocolate? Medical studies have proved that beyond a shadow of a doubt. Let's stop by Popeye's. My treat."

Angie relaxed. It was nice to be able to go to Popeye's with Jack and not have to worry that Marcos would find out and give her all kinds of grief. And Jack seemed to have backed off from wanting romance and to have settled for friendship. She hadn't realized how much energy she'd spent battling with Marcos. It was a tremendous relief to finally be able to focus on what *she* really wanted.

Now, as they sat in a booth, Jack held up his mug. "*Salud, amor, y pesetas*," he began, struggling a little with the Spanish words.

"*Y el tiempo para gozarlos*," she finished for him quickly. "'Health, love, and money, and the time to enjoy them.' Your Spanish is really improving, Jack."

"*De nada*," he said, lowering his eyes modestly. "It's nothing."

The toast reminded her of her conversation with

Connie, her stepmother. *Why not?* she thought and plunged ahead. "I was wondering if you'd like to go to a fiesta next weekend at the Hispanic Heritage Center. My stepmother has a part in a play, and she says there's going to be food and music and everything. It ought to be fun."

Jack stared at her in mock disbelief and banged on the side of his head. "Can I trust my ears? Is Angela Montoya actually inviting Juan Mertz to a fiesta? Anyway, my answer is *si*."

"Let's take a break," Lan said, and Adam instantly agreed. For an hour they had been practicing in Adam's bedroom, a small, neat room with bunk beds and a map of the world covering one wall. They were working on the piece Adam had to prepare for the re-audition. There was no way Lan was ever going to make Adam into a real musician, but with the constant repetition it seemed likely that Adam would at least be able to stay on with the Youth Symphony.

As soon as they stopped, there was a light tap at Adam's door and Mrs. Wolf peeked in. "That sounded just wonderful," she said, smiling. "You must be ravenously hungry after all that hard work. Dinner's ready whenever you are."

"Let's eat," Adam said, and Lan followed him to the kitchen.

Four places had been set at the round wooden table, and Mrs. Wolf was ladling soup into pottery bowls. The Wolfs' house was not at all what Lan expected—it was small and homey, rather than large and luxurious. "This is Nigerian peanut soup," she explained. "I hope you like it. It's a favorite of my boys."

"Where's the Squid?" Adam asked. At that moment a boy of about twelve with a sprinkling of freckles across his nose came into the kitchen, and Adam introduced his brother. "This is Jedediah," he said. "I call him the Squid, but he prefers Jed."

Jed and Lan solemnly shook hands, and Mrs. Wolf brought a loaf of still-warm homemade bread and a large wedge of cheese to the table. "It looks great," Lan said appreciatively as they all sat down. "I think you must like to cook."

She smiled and started to answer, but Jed interrupted. "Where's Daddy?" he asked. Her smile faded.

"He won't be home until late tonight," she said briskly.

"Again?" Jed asked plaintively.

Mrs. Wolf's smile seemed to slip ever so slightly. "This is a very busy time in your father's office, Jed. We'll just go ahead and eat without him, shall we?"

"As usual," Lan heard Adam mutter under his breath.

"Well, Lan, it sounds like you have a very busy schedule. You're going to your job at Red's after dinner, aren't you?" Mrs. Wolf seemed determined to overlook her sons' discontent.

"Yes, ma'am," Lan said politely. He tasted the thick soup. "This is delicious," he told her.

"Mom's a great cook," Adam said, passing the bread to Lan. "She teaches geography, and we always get to eat something from whatever country she's teaching."

"Africa this week, right, Mom?" Jed asked.

"Right. China's next. I teach at the Academy, Lan," Mrs. Wolf explained.

"That's how the Squid and I ended up there," Adam said.

"Nathaniel did too, but he didn't like it," Jed informed Lan. "So he went to Roosevelt, like you."

Lan barely had time to finish his apple pie—

84

"Dessert is always American," Mrs. Wolf explained—before he and Adam had to leave to get Lan to work on time for the evening shift.

"Okay," Adam said as they were headed toward Red's in Nathaniel's Jeep, "what about these driving lessons we were talking about? If we're going to do this legally, you have to get a learner's permit. Or I can just take you out to a vacant lot and show you what to do and let you drive around there for a while. It's up to you."

"I want a license," Lan said definitely, not knowing until that moment that it was important to him, that it mattered at all. "So I'll go get a permit."

"Great. When do you want to start?"

"How about Friday?" Lan said. "I don't have to work. And I'll have the permit by then."

Several times during that evening while he was working, Lan thought about Adam and his family. They seemed like such nice people. But Lan was disappointed. He had been hoping that Adam would have another two hundred dollars to pay him on the viola, but Adam had said nothing and Lan felt a little guilty even thinking about it—Mrs. Wolf had been so kind to him, telling him he was welcome there any time, wrapping up a couple of slices of the bread and a generous piece of cheese to take with him. Except for Nathaniel, Adam's family didn't seem to be rich at all. And right now, Nathaniel apparently wasn't rich enough to pay for the viola.

And then there was that strange conversation they had had on their way to Adam's house in the Jeep. Adam had asked how the hotline was going, and Lan had said fine, lots of interesting calls, and Adam had launched into a long description about a friend of his from school. "There's this kid at school who's in a whole lot of trouble," Adam had said. "Actually the *kid* isn't, but his brother is. The brother is a major drug dealer, but no one knows it. The kid's whole family is totally screwed up, though, and nobody knows that either—everyone thinks they're Mr. and Mrs. Happy Family." He'd tapped his fingers moodily on the steering wheel. "The brother does drugs, too. And it's messing this kid up. He's really worried about his brother."

"We've been getting a lot of calls like that," Lan had said. "Drugs are a terrible problem that seems to be getting worse. I just don't see how any human being can get mixed up in anything like that. I can't understand it and I really don't have any sympathy for people who do drugs. Or people who sell drugs. They're not just hurting themselves, but they're hurting their families and everyone who cares about them."

And then Adam had changed the subject, back to the Youth Symphony, and they had talked about the reauditions until they arrived at Adam's house.

Now Lan replayed the conversation in his head. It sounded a lot like the calls they had been getting from Ninja. Too much. Was it possible that Adam's friend and Ninja were the same person? It really didn't matter if Adam knew Ninja, he decided. But if Adam needed to talk about his friend's problem, Lan would be there to listen.

"I need your advice, Nikki," Kurt told her. "Can we get together and talk? I think I've got a real problem."

"Oh, I have no trouble believing *that*," Nikki said, laughing. Kurt could picture her balanced on a stool by the phone in her kitchen, scrunching her fingers in her short, curly hair and teasing him. "You have a knack for problems, Kurt."

"And you have a knack for bailing me out," he said,

going along with her good-natured kidding, although he was far from matching Nikki's jovial mood. "You want to go somewhere?"

"Sure. I'm sick of homework. I could use a muffin break at Red's."

Fifteen minutes later Kurt picked her up at the mobile home park where she lived with her mother. By the time they got to Red's, giant snowflakes were floating down lazily. "I wish this would turn into a real blizzard," Nikki said, pulling off her knitted cap and mittens. "I'm ready for some cross-country skiing. Would you be interested, maybe next weekend?"

Kurt shook his head. "I'm a downhill man myself." He remembered the ski trip to Colorado with his parents over the Christmas holidays. At first Kurt hadn't wanted to go with them, to miss all the parties in Eldorado, and to spend that much time with his family. But it had worked out fine. The powder snow was deep and lush, and he and his father were out on the slopes every day. His father was a good skier, and Kurt found himself actually enjoying his father's company.

"I wonder if Lan's working tonight," Nikki said when the waitress had brought their coffee and Red's Special, a basket of assorted muffins. "I should have asked her."

"He'd probably be too busy to come out and talk anyway," Kurt said. He buttered a poppy seed muffin. "Do you get the feeling Lan's life is a lot more complicated than we realize?"

"Actually I never thought about it, but I bet you're right. He keeps everything under control, so it always looks pretty simple. But I have a feeling it's not Lan you want to talk about."

"You're right, Nik. It's Michelle. Something's really wrong there, and I don't know what to do about it."

Kurt described the scene in the restaurant and Nikki's eyes widened as he told her about Michelle's behavior. "So she has a drug problem that started with her mom's diet pills. She's probably buying speed on the street now, though—it's easy to get, and cheap, too. The thing is, she still insists that she doesn't have a problem, even though it's obvious."

Nikki listened silently to his story. "I kind of figured something like that. For instance, when she got so upset at the idea of the hotline taking an anti-drug pledge. She was so far out of line on that."

"So what do I do, Nikki? It's practically impossible to help somebody who won't even admit she has a problem."

"I don't know." Nikki broke open a muffin and studied the blueberries. "She needs friends, that's for sure. I think she really needs you to be there for her. I'm not sure she'll accept any help from me, but I'll try. Will you be seeing her again soon, do you think?"

"I don't know," Kurt said. "You know, after that whole scene, it turns out that Rachel Steinway won't even be around for the Mayor's Ball. I still can't take Michelle, though."

"I can't believe that Michelle honestly expected you to take her to the ball after . . . after everything that came out during the campaign," Nikki said carefully. "It's just another example of what drugs do. Her judgement is completely shot; she has no sense of perspective on this thing."

"She says hardly anybody would know she's Maureen Piper's daughter, that they wouldn't run it on the ten o'clock news. Or even that anybody would *care*."

"So what *are* you going to do, Kurt?"

88

"I figured I'd just show up in a tux and dance once with my mom and that would be it."

"I mean about Michelle. Her drug problem. Because we've got to think of something, before it's too late."

PART III

Ninja

Tuesday, January 9

"**W**ho's on this afternoon?"

"I am," Jenny answered.

"Who's your partner?" Ilana asked. "As if I didn't know."

"Me," said Rob.

"I wonder," Steven pondered aloud, "if it's a good idea to always have the same partner. Especially when it's someone you see so much away from the hotline."

"Why *wouldn't* it be a good idea, Steven?" Jenny asked. "Obviously if we stay with the same partner, it's because we trust that person to pick up on our signals."

"I might bring it up at our meeting on Wednesday," Steven said. "Get some more opinions on this."

"I can't imagine who'd agree with you, Steven," Ilana said. "I never do."

"Of course not. You're my sister. My point is that the hotline is not a dating game. I think if Jenny and Rob are always on duty together, they'll tend to pay more attention to each other than they will to the callers."

Ilana folded her arms and glared at her brother. "My

opinion, Steven, is that you want to keep things mixed up so that you will have a chance to be partners with Kristen Hallett. *She* may not have noticed your worshipful glances, but *I* have."

Jenny sighed. The Feldmans were at it again with their sibling rivalry. Ilana loved to puncture Steven's pompous balloon with her sharp barbs, but she had really left herself open this time. Jenny braced for Steven's attack, sure he'd bring up Ilana's ridiculous crush on Mr. Montgomery. Jenny kept hoping Ilana would drop it and get interested in someone her own age, someone *appropriate*. But, incredibly, Steven let that go by.

"What about your worshipful glances at Jason Aragon, Ilana?" he countered. "You practically salivate every time he comes into the hotline room."

Jenny's jaw dropped. Jason Aragon? Jenny hadn't noticed that Ilana was paying special attention to one of the new hotliners, and Ilana had never said word one about him. But before Jenny could hear Ilana's reply, the phone rang and Jenny rushed to take the first call on her shift.

"Hello," the caller said politely. "This is Ninja. I talked to a couple of people there last week. Is it okay if I call again?"

"Sure," Jenny said, scrambling in the desk drawer for the hotline log and something to write with. "Call as often as you need to talk. That's what we're here for."

In the heavy silence that followed, Jenny flipped back to last week's log and found Kurt's entry on Thursday: *Ninja:—older bro. uses, deals drugs—little bro. worships—parents don't know—worried.* On the next page, Friday, Kristen Hallett had noted: *Ninja, 2nd call, still upset about brother.*

"Hello?" she said. "Are you still there, Ninja?"

"I'm still here," he answered.

"Has anything happened since you called last week?" Jenny asked.

"Well, yes and no. Nothing's really happened yet, but I have this awful feeling, you know? Like something could go wrong any minute and the whole thing come crashing down."

"You mean your brother?"

"Yeah. I guess I've known for a long time that he's been into drugs, and I haven't wanted to deal with it. But I worry about him, that he's going to get killed, or busted, or something. But he's so cool, see, so good at it, that I sometimes think he'll probably never get caught. He doesn't have a hot car, no BMW or Corvette, just a plain old Jeep. And no big, expensive apartment either. He rents a run-down old house near the university. He has one bedroom set up like a fitness center, and my younger brother loves to go over there and work out, because nobody hassles him."

Ninja stopped talking. Jenny waited. "So what are you afraid of, if everything's so cool?" she prodded finally.

"It's the guys he works for, the Trio. Those three guys run one of the biggest drug operations here in town. My brother supplies the main dealers in some of the dormitories at the university. That's kind of his specialty. They call him the Professor. He got into it while he was still a student, before he dropped out. Anyway, he's the link between the Trio that gets the stuff from Colombia or Mexico, and the dorm captains, I guess you could call them. The captains pay my brother, and my brother pays the Trio. I guess as long as everything is working out okay, it's fine."

"And you're afraid things aren't working out okay?"

"Yeah. Right. Like the captains aren't paying or something, and my brother doesn't have the money for the Trio."

"Ninja, how did you find out all this? Did your brother tell you?"

"Most of it. One night he was really high, and he told me the whole story. Another thing I found out is what happens if something goes wrong. Sunday night the Trio picked up a guy my brother knows, somebody who was putting so much of his inventory up his own nose that he couldn't pay up what he owed, and they worked him over pretty bad. Beat him up and dumped him in Riverbend Park. The guy almost died, until somebody came by and found him and took him to the hospital. The thing is, I'm scared something like that is going to happen to my brother."

"Oh, God." Jenny wiped her clammy hands on her jeans. "Have you tried to talk to your brother, Ninja? To tell him how scared you are?"

"I *have* tried, but—" Abruptly his tone changed. "Gotta go. Somebody's here. Thanks."

The line went dead. Jenny stared at the phone. "I think that's one of the worst I've had." She told Rob about the Trio and Ninja's fears for his brother. "And he sounds so nice. He shouldn't have to go through all this. I wish there was some way to help him! I don't even know what to *say*."

"Having somebody to listen to him is probably a big help. I thought you handled that all very well, Jenny, even though it was hard."

"Thank you." She smiled at him shakily and reached for his hand, feeling a rush of warmth. "Oh, Rob . . ." she began, leaning toward him.

It was inevitable, she realized, that Steven Feldman would choose exactly that moment to open the door from the outer office and catch them gazing at each other, their lips only inches apart.

Jenny straightened up self-consciously, hot with embarrassment. "Okay, Steven," she sighed. "You're right. You win."

Wednesday, January 10

"It starts out with this guy telling me how depressed he feels," Jason Aragon was saying, "how he's mad all the time, and sometimes he thinks about killing himself. Then he gives me this story about how *small* he is, sixteen years old and only five-seven and weighs one-twenty-one, and he's sick of it. So he starts taking steroids to make himself bigger. He says he knows a lot of jocks, weight-lifters and so on, who take them, and they really work. In a few weeks he puts on a lot of bulk. But as soon as he quits taking them, it all goes away. So now he wants to go back on them. But you know the real reason he called? Because he knows a black market dealer, but it's pretty expensive, and he wants to know if I can tell him where to find a job so he can buy the stuff!"

Lan's attention had been wandering. He was trying to figure out how he was going to ride out to the Motor Vehicle Department for his learner's permit and make it back to Havilands to do his Wednesday cooking stint. But the mention of steroids caught his attention.

He had heard rumors that they were being sold around school, but he didn't know much about them.

"But they're incredibly dangerous!" Jenny remarked. "Did you tell him how dangerous steroids are, Jason?"

"I sure did. I told him that's why he was feeling depressed all the time—roids do that to you—but he didn't believe me. Then I rattle off a list of the side effects—liver damage, heart damage, kidney damage—and he's going 'yeah, yeah, ho hum.' Then I mention that he might go bald and his acne is definitely going to get worse, and he doesn't have much to say. Then I hit him with the big one: 'Your balls are going to shrink. You're going to be a great big man with itty bitty balls.' And the kid says, 'You're full of it, man, you're just making that stuff up to scare me.' And I say, I'm not making anything up, it's all true, and then I tell him I know how he feels, because I'm not very big and I'm never going to be very big, but I'm not going to ruin the body I do have with stuff like that."

"Sounds as though you covered it all," Mr. Montgomery said. "You're very well informed on the subject, and you certainly gave it to him straight."

Jason looked sheepish. "I got all that information the hard way," he confessed. "I used to take roids, too. And then I heard a sports doctor at the university medical center talk about all the things that can happen to you. It scared the hell out of me, and I decided that's it, no way."

"Lucky for him that he got you, Jason," Lan said. "I wouldn't have known what to say because I don't know anything about it."

"What *would* you have said, Lan?" Nikki asked curiously. "If you didn't know anything about steroids, how would you have handled that call?"

Lan thought over her question. "It sounds as though he doesn't like himself much, so I might have talked about that. Then I'd have suggested maybe he could study kung fu, where *looking* powerful isn't important at all. It's discipline that matters, more than muscle."

"Self-image is a problem for a lot of people," Steven said. "Particularly adolescents."

"Oh, *tell* us about it, Dr. Feldman," Ilana said with a giggle.

"Boys want to be taller and have bigger muscles, and girls want to be thinner and have bigger breasts," Steven replied, apparently unperturbed by his sister's needling, "not realizing that it's all in the genes. That's G-E-N-E-S, Ilana."

Things did get nasty between Steven and Ilana, Lan noted. He had never had an argument with his sister, and even if he disagreed with her, he wouldn't dream of teasing her or talking to her disrespectfully. He knew that he and Sieu An would get along fine when she and Johnny moved into his apartment. He hoped it would be soon—that when she came to his place on Sunday, it would all be settled.

Ms. Hawkins broke up the Feldman family feud. "Steven does have a good point, though I question his manner of presenting it," she said. "Certainly Lan's approach, dealing with the caller's underlying problem, would have been valid, but I think we all learned a lot from Jason with his educational approach. Any other calls we need to discuss today?"

There were others—the girl whose parents were threatening to send her to boarding school if her grades didn't improve, the boy whose father was getting married to a woman the boy didn't like. Calls were still coming in from people wanting to talk about Joseph and Karen, whose funerals had taken place over the weekend. But the big one was Jenny's call from Ninja.

"This guy is so scared for his brother," she said after she had reconstructed the conversation. "And his brother must be a totally selfish, drugged-out jerk not to realize what he's doing to his family."

"That's another thing about drugs," Mr. Montgomery said. "It blows holes in your common sense. It turns basically decent people into self-centered idiots. They'll deny there's any problem right to the very end."

"And the end could be in a prison cell or a hospital bed," Kristen said.

"Or a slab in the morgue with a tag on your toe," Jason added.

Lan shuddered, and for a minute no one said a word.

Then someone mentioned semester finals coming up in a week, and someone else wondered if they would be running the hotline during exam week. Jenny, naturally, protested that kind of thinking. "I'll be taking my shift," she said, "and I'd be glad to do anybody else's who's too busy." But there were no takers on her offer.

As soon as the meeting ended, Lan got ready to begin the long haul out to Motor Vehicles and said goodbye to April, who was seated at the hotline desk for her shift. "Call me, Lan," she said, and he promised he would.

"Lan, I can't believe you did this," Jenny protested. "All you had to say was, 'I want to go to the Motor Vehicles Department,' and we could have put your bike in the truck and taken you. It would have saved you hours. I don't know how you even manage to get around at all in this weather. Promise you'll let us drive you home after dinner tonight, okay?"

"Okay, Jenny. But I don't want to put you to any trouble."

"Lan, it's really no trouble," Rob said. He had accepted Jenny's mother's invitation to stay for dinner, since his parents were in Los Angeles.

"We want to do it, honestly," Jenny said. *Lan, the mystery man,* Jenny thought. *I'll probably never understand what's going on in his head.* Now, for instance, he had ridden practically across the city to get his learner's permit. Why today? And who was going to teach him to drive?

She wanted to ask him a lot of other questions, too, like what it was like living in his own apartment, and how he was managing with all his jobs. Jenny had the feeling that something wasn't quite right—like maybe Lan was in over his head. But Lan was concentrating on cooking tonight's meal. And Rob thought she asked too many questions anyway. Maybe he was right. She'd have to wait.

"I didn't know you were planning to learn to drive, Lan," Rob said. "Who's teaching you?"

Jenny stifled a giggle. So Rob was as curious as she was!

"A friend from the Youth Symphony," Lan explained. He was whirling something in the blender, and he spoke so softly that Jenny could scarcely hear him above the noise.

"Who?" Jenny asked when the blender stopped.

"Adam."

"Adam? The guy who bought Lissa's viola?" She saw

102

Rob's eyebrow arch disapprovingly, and she corrected herself. "I mean, *your* viola."

"Yes."

Now she was filled with questions. Why Adam Wolf, of all people? Jenny would have been glad to teach Lan to drive. Or her father could have taught him; he was a good teacher, and he really liked Lan. The whole time he was living here, he could have been learning. But instead Lan had to go his own way, pick somebody like this Adam Wolf. If Rob weren't here, she would have kept after Lan until she had pried the facts out of him. Instead she asked, "Is there anything we can do to help you with dinner?"

"No, thanks, Jenny. It should be ready in a few minutes."

Since Jenny's parents were watching the evening news on television in the solar room, Jenny and Rob went into the living room to talk. She heard the phone ring and her father call to Lan.

"It's driving you crazy, isn't it?" Rob asked teasingly. "Not knowing exactly what Lan is up to?"

"I wouldn't say that," Jenny protested, although she knew Rob was right. "It's Adam Wolf that bothers me. Who is he? Do we know anything about him?"

"Why should we know anything about him, besides what Lan's told us?"

"I don't know," Jenny grumbled. "I just wish I did, that's all."

Lan picked up the extension phone in the kitchen. "Hi, it's Adam," the husky voice said. "I've got some money for you. I could bring it to you this evening, wherever you say."

"Can you bring it to my apartment later?" Lan asked. He did a quick calculation; Jenny had offered to take him home in the truck, so he'd be there a little earlier. "Eight-thirty?"

"Sure," Adam said. "See you there."

When dinner was over, Rob and Jenny began to clean up the dishes. "Let us know when you're ready to go," Jenny said.

"I'd like to make a phone call first," Lan said, remembering his promise to April. "Is it all right if I use the phone?" he asked diffidently.

"Well of *course* it's all right," Jenny replied. "This is still your home, you know."

Lan ducked his head in acknowledgment. It was nice of her to say that, but he had never really thought of this as home, Lan realized as he dialed April's number. Moments later there was April's bubbly voice, telling him all about the calls that had come in on her shift, including another one from Ninja.

"You know, that boy really spooks me!" she said. "'Nobody knows the truth about me,' he said. 'They all think I have this wonderful life, and you guys on the hotline are the only ones I can really be honest with. Everybody else gets the lies.' And then he starts talking about his brother again."

"What's happening with him?"

"Ninja says his brother's definitely in big trouble. A couple of the guys who work for him have disappeared, and they haven't paid what they owe him—so the brother doesn't have the money to pay off the Trio, that's what he calls his bosses. And he's got only a few days to get the money, or really terrible things are going to happen to him."

"Did he say what kind of terrible things?"

"No. But I just know it must be *bad,* because it's a lot of money. And these guys sound pretty ruthless." Lan heard her voice drift away as she spoke to someone else. Then she came back on the phone. "Gotta go. My dad needs the phone. Bye."

"Bye, April." Lan checked the clock on Mr. Haviland's desk. If Jenny and Rob took him home now, he might have time to get a few things done before Adam arrived. He felt as if he was falling farther and farther behind. He'd already given up Youth Symphony, and he didn't want to let anything else go. It had been weeks now, for instance, since he had practiced his kung fu, and he knew he'd feel better—physically and mentally—if he got back into it again.

But Jenny was slow getting organized, and then she promised her father she'd stop for gas on the way, and Lan knew there would be no time to do anything before Adam arrived. In fact Adam might even get there ahead of them. He hoped not; Lan really didn't want to have to introduce Adam to Jenny. She hadn't said anything about the viola, but Lan knew it still bothered her a lot that he had sold it to Adam.

But Lan saw the black motorcycle parked in front of his building when they pulled in, and the tall boy with a helmet cradled in the crook of his arm waved when he recognized Lan in the truck. "Looks like somebody's been waiting for you," Rob said.

"Who is it?" Jenny asked, switching off the ignition. "Adam."

Lan jumped out of the car before Jenny could react. Adam pulled off his leather glove and shook hands with Rob and Jenny when Lan introduced them.

"So how're you doing with the viola?" Jenny asked, and Lan noticed that she managed to call it "the viola" and not "Lissa's viola." That was progress.

"Pretty good, thanks to Lan," Adam replied with a broad smile.

Rob sauntered over and peered at Adam's motorcy-

105

cle. "Great-looking machine," he said admiringly. "Looks powerful."

"It *is* powerful—maybe a little too much for me," Adam admitted. "It's actually my brother's."

Lan and Jenny strolled over to take a closer look. It was a handsome bike, Lan had to admit, with its sleek black fairing lettered in gold: Kawasaki Twin-Cam 16-Valve. Then he walked around the back of the motor-cycle and froze. The racy script on the tailpipe leaped out at him: NINJA. *Ninja*? Was there a connection, or was this just a coincidence?

Lan's brain raced to add up what he knew about Ninja and Adam: older brothers, younger brothers, money problems. It *could* be a coincidence, he concluded; but his gut told him it wasn't.

Careful to keep his face expressionless, Lan glanced at Adam, who was continuing to discuss the merits of the motorcycle with Rob. Lan hadn't mentioned that these were friends from the hotline, and Adam—if he really was Ninja—would have no way of knowing that he had actually talked to Jenny yesterday afternoon. Unless he recognized her voice. Unless she had told him her name.

Lan shifted his glance to Jenny. Lan could almost *see* her making the connection: her blue eyes widened, and her mouth opened. Then she closed her mouth again. Lan looked away, resolutely refusing to meet her stare. *Don't let her say anything*, Lan wished fervently; *let me figure out how to handle this*.

It seemed like forever until Jenny and Rob finally climbed back into the truck and drove away, and Lan led Adam up to his apartment, still uncertain what to say or do next.

Adam set his helmet on a chair and unzipped his jacket. "Lan, listen," he said, licking his lips nervously. "I got you a few bucks. Not as much as I had hoped, but at least it's something." He pulled a tightly rolled wad of bills out of a zippered pocket. "It's only a hundred. I have to tell you I borrowed it from Jed. He's the one in the family who's really good about saving money!" Adam managed a laugh. "But anyway, my brother's really in a tight spot these days—even Jed can't help him out! But it won't be long now. I'm pretty sure—"

Lan cut him off. "It's okay, Adam," he said. "I can wait."

His mind was still churning. *But can I really afford to wait? April said Ninja's brother owed a whole lot of money and was in a whole lot of trouble . . . if this is Ninja . . . and if it is, I might never get that money.*

"Thanks, Lan," Adam said, the relief plain in his voice. "I really appreciate that. Now, when do you want that driving lesson?" He sounded almost jovial. "How about tomorrow?"

"Tomorrow," Lan agreed. *Maybe by tomorrow I'll know what to say. And how to say it.*

"That's him," Jenny said, putting the truck into reverse. "That's Ninja. No question."

"Ninja?" Rob asked. "You think Adam Wolf is Ninja? How did you manage to come up with that one, Jenny?"

"I saw the name of his bike. *Ninja.* You must have seen it, too, Rob. We can go back and look at it, if you don't believe me. Obviously he's taken the name of his bike as his code name for the hotline."

"It's not obvious to me at all, Jenny. 'Ninja' could stand for just about anything. It wouldn't have to be a motorcycle. I think you need a lot more evidence than that to conclude that Adam Wolf is Ninja."

"Don't forget I talked to him on the phone yesterday. I'm sure I recognized his voice."

"Really? He didn't say that much, did he? And people sound different on the phone than they do in person."

"I'm positive," Jenny insisted. "Anyway, Lan knows, I'll bet you anything. I'm going to ask him about it first thing tomorrow."

Thursday, January 11

"**O**kay, Adam, let's take that section again." Lan tapped the music with his bow, to show where he wanted Adam to start. "It's coming, but we're not there yet."

The whole thing was insane, Lan thought. They were like actors in a play, performing roles: Lan, the patient teacher; Adam, the hard-working pupil. And those roles had absolutely nothing to do with what was going on in their real lives.

Besides, what Lan said was a lie. The section wasn't improving, and when they went through it two more times it got even worse. It was clear to Lan that Adam couldn't concentrate, that he was putting most of his energy into staying in control.

Or was Lan just imagining all this stuff about Adam? Could Adam really be Ninja and have the problem that Ninja had? Yesterday Lan had been certain. Today he wasn't quite so sure. Jenny was, though. Lan wasn't at all surprised to find her waiting for him by his locker first thing this morning.

"Adam Wolf is Ninja," she had said. "How long have you known that?"

"I *don't* know it," Lan replied carefully.

"But you *think* he is, don't you?" she insisted. "Have you asked him?"

"No," he said, "I haven't. I've got a class now. Excuse me, Jenny." And he had hurried away. But he was certain that would not be the end of it.

He had dreaded stopping by the hotline room after school. Jenny was sure to be there, and he knew she might bring it up again. But—and this time he *was* surprised—she didn't. She had even less evidence than Lan did—and what difference would it make anyway? Still, he was grateful for her silence.

Whenever Adam talked about his family, Lan thought, it always sounded fine, the perfect all-American family, although it had begun to seem less perfect lately, with all the financial problems. Lan remembered how Adam and Jed had reacted to their father's absence at dinner last week. The fairy tale was developing some cracks, and through those cracks Lan thought he could glimpse the *real* family. Possibly Ninja's family.

But Lan still hadn't figured out a way to ask the right questions. For the time being, Lan decided, he would put Ninja out of his mind. There were other things to think about.

They played the section again. There was no use pretending that it had gotten any better.

"Let's take a break and go driving," Adam said finally. "I brought the Jeep, and I found a place not too far from here where you can practice."

"All right," Lan said.

Sitting in the driver's seat and following Adam's instructions, Lan put his foot on the clutch, shifted into

110

first gear, and slowly pressed on the gas pedal. Nothing happened.

"Keep feeding it gas," Adam advised. "And then *slowly* let out the clutch. You'll feel it catch."

Lan tried to do exactly as he was told. Adam was a good teacher, patient and thorough. It was a great feeling when he got accelerator and clutch synchronized and began to creep along in low gear. He was driving!

"You're doing great, Lan," Adam said. "Have you ever driven before?"

Lan shook his head. "I got a book from the library," he said seriously. "It explains the internal combustion engine, what happens in the cylinders, how power is transferred to the drive shaft. So I have a good start, I think."

Adam laughed. "You already know a lot more than I do," he said. "I figure if I can read the speedometer and the gas gauge, that's good enough."

For the next hour Lan concentrated on shifting from one gear to the next, up, down, faster, slower. It didn't matter much what he did about the steering, because he was making slow loops in a big, empty field. For that hour Lan managed to put out of his mind all of his concerns about Ninja. He simply drove.

"You should feel good about that, Lan," Adam said after the lesson ended and Adam was driving back to Lan's apartment. "We could open a school: 'The Nguyen and Wolf School of Music and Driving.' We'd probably make a fortune."

Lan smiled. "Are you feeling any better about Saturday's rehearsal?"

Adam groaned. "I guess I'm feeling okay about this Saturday, but two weeks from Saturday has me scared out of my mind. The auditions."

"The orchestra is really important to you, isn't it?"

Adam pulled into a parking place near Lan's apartment and turned off the engine. "Yeah. It is." He was staring straight ahead, rubbing his chin. "Or was."

Lan studied Adam for a long moment and made his decision: this was the time. He hadn't figured out a strategy, but maybe he didn't need one. He'd just plunge in. "Ninja?" Lan said softly.

Adam's head jerked around. "What?"

"Are you Ninja?"

"I don't know what you're talking about." But Lan knew by the look on Adam's face that it was true. Then: "What do you want to know for?" Adam's jaw was hard, and he turned away to stare out the window again.

"Maybe I could help you."

"What makes you think it's me?" Adam's voice sounded different to Lan, tense and scared.

"I saw the name of your motorcycle. And then it all started to add up."

Adam eased off a little. "Does it make any difference to you if I *am* Ninja?"

"I want to help. You're my friend. Ninja's hurting, so you're hurting. Besides," Lan said, groping his way along, "I've got a sister I worry about. I think she's in a lot of trouble, and I don't know what to do for her. So I know what it's like to feel helpless when someone you love needs help."

Finally Adam turned and faced him, pain showing in his blue eyes. "Your sister is into drugs?"

"No, not drugs." Lan pulled in a deep breath. "She's married to a man who . . . isn't good to her. She has a little boy. I rented this apartment so they'd have a safe place to stay. I worry about them. What hurts them hurts me, too." Lan felt his throat tighten, and he chewed on his lip.

112

Adam banged on the steering wheel. "Man, oh man, do I know what you're talking about. My brother is in so much trouble!"

"You want to tell me about it? I've heard some of it from April, and other people you've talked to on the hotline. But I need to hear it from you."

Adam covered his face with his hands. Lan thought he was crying, but when Adam let his hands fall into his lap, he seemed calm again, almost frozen. "Did they tell you about the Trio, the men in charge of the whole operation? Nathaniel works for them. He started dealing because it seemed a good way to get drugs for himself. Cocaine. It's funny—he's scared of crack. 'I don't want to get hooked on that stuff,' he says, like he's not hooked already on coke! But then it started getting bigger and bigger. I guess he started making a lot of bucks. He gave me the money for the viola. But then a lot of things started to go wrong. He lost a couple of his best dealers, the guys who work for him. Now all of a sudden he's deep in debt to the Trio, and unless he comes up with it, they'll work him over. Break his legs, I don't know what all. Not kill him— just wreck him."

"How do you know all this?" Lan asked quietly. "Did he tell you?"

"Yes!" The cry was wrenched out of him, as though he could actually feel his brother's physical pain. "Yes, he told me about it the other night. I went to ask him when I could have the rest of the money to give you, to finish paying for the viola. He says he's going to try to talk to them. He says it's only a matter of a couple of weeks until he can get it all put together again, line up some new 'dorm reps,' make back the money he owes. I just hope he can do it."

113

"You hope he can do it?" Lan repeated. "Where are you in all of this, Adam?"

"I'm with my brother," Adam said. "Where else would I be?"

"But what do you mean, you're with him? You go along with what he's doing?"

"Not exactly go along with it, but what do you expect me to do, Lan? Turn my back on him? Turn him in?"

"You could quit taking money from him," Lan said. "Stop using his motorcycle and his Jeep. That would let him know how you really feel about what he's doing. Turning him in would seem like you were being a traitor, but that's one way to get him away from the Trio. And it could blow the whole drug operation wide open. The police would protect him, and they might even let him off, a suspended sentence or something, in exchange for the information." Lan wasn't sure about that, but he thought it was possible.

"He could get killed if he does that," Adam said.

"He could get killed if he *doesn't*."

"I know," Adam said with a sigh.

"I have to tell you, Adam, that I'm really anti-drug. I think everybody who deals should be behind bars, so they can't destroy people's lives anymore." He wished he could have thought of some other way to say it—it sounded so cold, so unfeeling. As though he didn't care.

Adam was silent. "I see what you mean," he said at last. "But he's not your brother."

Lan fumbled for the door handle. "Thanks for the lesson," he said, climbing out of the Jeep. "I'll see you later." But Adam looked away, as if Lan wasn't even there.

Lan had scarcely closed the apartment door before

114

the realization hit home: it was Nathaniel's money that was paying for the viola. Lan was just as wrong as Adam. Indirectly, Lan was accepting drug money, too.

For the rest of the evening, Lan wrestled with the problem. Adam still owed him seven hundred dollars. But as desperately as Lan needed it, he was sure of one thing: he could not accept any more of the tainted money. And what about the money he had already received? Lan agonized, knowing that he should give it back, although much of it had already been spent. During the long night, Lan made up his mind to contact Adam and work out a plan. In the meantime, of course, Adam could keep the viola.

But there could be no more coaching. And Lan's driving lessons were over before they had really begun.

Friday, January 12

Lan ran the two blocks from the bus stop to Goodwill. "I'm late," he gasped. "I'm sorry. I've been trying to reach Adam."

But April seemed unperturbed. "That's okay," she said. "I've been here only a few minutes myself. And I've been looking at stuff in the window."

It was April's idea to meet at the Goodwill store to shop for extras for the apartment. Lan would never have thought of it—he knew the apartment needed a lot of things, although he wasn't sure exactly what. "You'd be surprised, Lan," she had said to him at lunch, "what a difference a couple little things would make. A pretty tablecloth on that ugly kitchen table would be nice. And maybe some throw pillows on the sofa."

"Throw pillows?" He had looked at her blankly.

She laughed. "I see you're not into interior decoration," she said. "You know—just some pretty pillows so that you see something besides the gross green flowers."

Lan agreed reluctantly; he didn't want to spend

116

even a dollar he didn't absolutely have to. "You're probably right. I just want it to look *nice,* so Sieu An will like it. She and Johnny are coming on Sunday. But remember, April, I have practically no money."

"I remember," she assured him. "I have a good nose for a bargain. Trust me. Stuff is really cheap here."

April led the way up and down the aisles, searching through the used merchandise on crowded shelves and overflowing counters. Occasionally she seized an item that looked promising and eyed it critically, putting most things back and passing her finds on to Lan for his approval. Lan tried to act interested, but the only things that really got his attention were the price tags.

Eventually April had found everything she wanted, and Lan had agreed to everything but a floor lamp. He could get along without that. April had been right, though. Lan was surprised at how little everything cost.

They stopped at a waffle stand near the bus stop for something to eat and sat at a sticky table, surrounded by their parcels.

"Your mind is about a million miles away," April said. "Is it Sieu An?"

"Partly," he admitted. "But to tell you the truth, something else is bothering me. This is confidential, okay?" he added. "Because it's really hotline stuff."

"Sure," April said, and she crossed her heart. She was wearing her fuzzy pink V-necked sweater and the little gold heart on the fine gold chain. He always had trouble keeping his eyes off that heart, and he was sure April knew it.

"That guy Ninja who's been calling?" he said. "It's really Adam Wolf."

117

"You're kidding! Adam's brother is dealing drugs and all that? And you didn't know that about him?"

"He told me a completely different story. It's really hard to believe. I even went there on Monday and had dinner with his mother and his little brother, and they seemed like a great family, a dream family. His mother is really nice and a wonderful cook. She teaches at the school where Adam and his little brother go. They're really friendly people. The only thing I noticed was that Adam's father wasn't there, and Adam and his little brother both seemed kind of unhappy about it. But that was all! And now it turns out that there are lots of problems, some that his parents don't even know about. Adam's pretty upset. He doesn't know what to do." *And neither do I,* Lan thought.

"But how did you find out?"

"When he came over Wednesday evening, he was riding his brother's motorcycle. It's a Ninja—that's the name of that model. It clicked, and I began thinking of all the other similarities. Then I asked him about it yesterday, and he didn't deny it."

"Poor Ninja! Poor Adam! It must be awful to want to help someone in your family so much—" Then Lan saw the expression change and soften in April's eyes. She took Lan's hand in both of hers. "Lan, I think I know one reason this is bothering you so much. You want your family together, too." She stopped, and Lan heard a catch in her voice. "You want to hear something funny? Not really funny, but sort of strange. That's what I want, too. Only it's never going to happen for me."

"Why, April?" He had the same feeling he had had with Adam—not knowing what to ask, or how to ask it.

"Because I've got a crazy family, too. My dad came

118

back from Vietnam, and I guess he was really pretty nuts. But my mother had waited for him, and they got married, and I was born, and then later my sisters were born. He got rid of his heroin addiction, but he was never quite right again. Anyway, about five years ago she gave up on him and decided to move to Alabama, and we were all supposed to come with her. Me and my two little sisters. But I just couldn't go and leave my dad all by himself, you know? He's better than he used to be, but he's still pretty weird. And I know it must have been hard for her to live with him. It's hard for *me* to live with him! So I told my mom she should take my sisters and go, and I'd come later. But I never went. Now she's got a new husband and they have two little boys, plus my sisters, and there wouldn't be room for me anyway, so . . ."

"It's okay, April," Lan said. For once he was the one who hugged *her*, in public. He felt bad for her, but he wished all of this didn't remind him of his own family, of the father who died on the beach in Vietnam getting Lan on the refugee boat, and the little brother who died on that boat, and the older brother he never saw again. Families blown apart and scattered all over the world, it seemed.

"So what are we going to do about Adam?" she asked sadly. "I'd sure hate to be in his situation."

"I don't know," Lan admitted. He didn't feel ready to tell her about the money crisis this was causing. "But I think we'd better get this stuff back to the apartment before it gets much later."

Lan noticed the Jeep as they took the shortcut around the end of the building and into the parking lot. He was sure it was the one Adam had been teaching him to drive—same dented fender, same first three digits on the license plate. Was Adam waiting for him? But why was it parked here, at the end of the building, instead of around in front, where Adam usually parked?

He decided not to say anything to April, who seemed to have regained her good humor, but he did manage to pass close enough to the Jeep to see that no one was sitting in it. While April was happily arranging the new pillows and tablecloth, Lan stepped into the bathroom. Something was going on in the apartment downstairs, and Lan tried not to listen to the angry male voices he could hear plainly. For a moment he thought he recognized one of the voices; it sounded like Adam. Could Adam be downstairs? Or Nathaniel? What was going on?

The questions haunted him for the rest of the evening; he was certain that either Adam or Nathaniel was downstairs. The panel truck, the black sedan, and the sports car were all parked in front, so Lan assumed that the huge, shirtless man, the thin man with the mustache, and the man in the ski jacket were down there, too.

He could not resist peering through the slats of the blinds to see if the cars were still in the parking lot. April noticed, of course. "What are you looking for, Lan?" she asked.

He didn't want to frighten her. "I wondered if it was snowing," he said.

They were all gone when he took April home. So was the Jeep. When he came back some time later, the cars were back, but no Jeep. Lan was relieved.

It could be anybody down there, Lan told himself. But he didn't really believe that. He knew who they were: the Trio.

Saturday, January 13

"**I**'ve got something to tell you, Kurt," Nikki said.

They were in the service area at Lundquist European Motors, where Kurt was tinkering with an ancient MG. Usually Nikki perched on a tall metal stool, watching him, and Kurt kept on working while she talked, but something in her tone of voice made him put down his tools and pay attention. "What is it, Nik?"

"I had a visit last night," she said. "From Michelle."

"Michelle came to see *you*?"

"She wanted to talk. She's too embarrassed to come to you, even though she knows she has to do that. She feels horrible about what happened at the restaurant the other night. And she admits she has a drug problem. It did start with her mom's diet pills—she got to like the high she was getting, she was really charged up, and the weight was coming off. When she was afraid her mom was catching on, she started buying from a kid at school. She told me she never felt better in her life—or worse. And then when we all started ragging her about how awful she looked, skinny and all, the only way she could cope with *that* was more pills. But now she's ready to quit. Only it isn't going to be easy."

"My God," Kurt breathed. "She told you all this?"

"Yeah. Crying all the time. Me holding her, her bawling her head off. She ended up staying all night at my place. When she finally stopped crying, my mother actually tried to get her to eat something! I was so afraid Michelle would lose it again. She's really fragile, Kurt."

Kurt was nearly speechless. "Do you think she'll go into a treatment program?" he asked when he had found his voice. "Or what?"

"I told her I'd help her find out about Narcotics Anonymous," Nikki said. "They've got a chapter here in town. I said I'd go with her at first, if she needed me to. But eventually she's got to do it on her own."

He knew he'd never have been able to cope with this the way Nikki did. "What do you think I should do?"

"Wait for her to call you, and then make it as easy for her as you can. I promised her we'd stick by her. I think for now she's okay. She promised me she wouldn't take any more pills, but I don't know how long she'll be able to resist. The high she gets must be pretty powerful. Now you can get back to your carburetor—I have to go help my mom clean house. By the way, it would be really good if you'd come with us to the NA meeting on Tuesday."

Kurt nodded. If there was one thing he really didn't want to do, it was go to an NA meeting. But if it would help Michelle, he'd do it.

"*Mind* if you come over, Rob?" Jenny chuckled. "Are you kidding? I'd be extremely *happy* if you'd come

122

over. Mom and Dad both went over to the campus, and I'm trying to talk myself into studying for exams next week. Also I promised Mom I'd do the laundry."

"I'll be right over," Rob told her.

Jenny dumped the wicker basket full of dirty clothes onto the floor and began sorting. She could at least get one load into the washer before Rob arrived. Then maybe she could try to do something about the way she looked. Ratty sweats and messy hair were not what Jenny wanted to greet Rob in.

As she quickly changed into jeans and a striped shirt, she thought about how Rob had sounded on the phone. *Kind of funny,* now that she played it over again in her head. *Maybe he's just feeling a little cramped now that his parents are back,* she reasoned.

Just as she was fastening the silver hair clip in place, the doorbell rang.

"Come on in," she said a little impatiently as Rob continued to stand on the doorstep looking at her. "Let's see what there is to eat," she called over her shoulder as Rob followed her into the house.

"You're in luck," she told him as she rummaged inside the refrigerator. "There are decent leftovers for a change—we had take-out last night. . . . Rob, what on earth are you looking at?" She'd turned around to find him still staring at her.

"You. I think," he said soberly, "that you are really beautiful, Jenny."

The tone of his voice grabbed her attention finally. She looked at him closely. Her heart lurched. "Rob, what is it? Is something wrong?"

"Yes and no."

"Tell me."

"I will," he said. "In a minute."

She didn't know what to do or say. She waited

123

quietly, letting the cold air pour out of the open refrigerator. She didn't care; Rob's words—and his tone of voice—made her feel hot all over.

Rob shook his head as if to clear it. "My parents came back from L.A. last night with terrific news—terrific for them and in some ways terrific for me, too, but also not so terrific. They've been hunting for a project that would take them overseas, to Europe or somewhere. My dad has some old connections in Czechoslovakia, and they've been invited to do a big project with the Czech film industry. The thing is, Jenny, I'm going, too. There's a chance for me to work with some film animators, which is something I've always been interested in, plus the fact that Prague is photographer's heaven, and . . ."

Jenny could hear the excitement building in Rob's voice as he talked on and on—the chance to see another country, to learn something so unusual, something so entirely different. She felt his enthusiasm, but she could also feel her throat tightening. "How long would you be gone?" she managed to ask in what she hoped sounded like a calm, normal voice.

"About six months," he said. "Maybe longer. But I'd come back in time to start college next fall."

Six months. Maybe longer. Jenny struggled to take in this news. "When?" It was all she could do to whisper this one word.

"Two weeks. Maybe three. It'll take that long to get our passports and visas and so on, although they started that process a while back, in case this came through."

"You've known about this before? And you never said a word?"

Rob leaned on the table. "I didn't think it would actually happen. And if it did happen, it wouldn't be this soon. More like the end of May or something. And I wasn't sure I'd actually go with them—at first they thought maybe I should just stay here and finish. But then this animation school came up, and the chance to do some photography—I might even do a photo essay on Czech teenagers. Something like what we did on the Youth Symphony."

"It sounds like you're really happy about going."

"Is it possible to feel two opposite ways at once? Sure I want to go—how many American kids ever get a chance to do something like this? But I don't want to leave here. Mostly I don't want to leave you. That's the part that hurts, Jenny. It really does. You understand that, don't you?" He was almost pleading with her.

Jenny did understand. She also understood that there wasn't any good part in this for her, not the way there was for him. And she couldn't pretend that it didn't hurt a lot. But there would be no breaking down in front of him, no weeping and carrying on. She squared her shoulders and blinked back tears. "I think it's great, Rob," she began, but then her voice broke. Rob reached out, his eyes glistening, and took her in his arms, and she leaned against his shoulder and let the tears come.

On her first afternoon as a waitress at Red's Diner, April brought a message to Lan in the kitchen. "Adam's out there," she said in a low voice. "He says he knows you're busy, but he wants to talk to you. He says he can wait until you have a break. What shall I tell him?"

Lan glanced at the clock on the wall. "Tell him I'll be out in about fifteen minutes," he said and went to work on the next order.

He found Adam hunched over a mug of coffee and

125

pulled out the chair across from Adam. No motorcycle helmet, so he must be driving the Jeep today, Lan thought. "Hello, Adam," he said.

"How's it going?" Adam asked, attempting a grin.

"All right." He waited. "You wanted to talk to me?"

"Yeah. Just to check in and let you know the rehearsal went pretty good today. At least Ellis didn't chew me out. Also," he said, reaching into his pocket, "I wanted to bring you this." He dropped a thick roll of bills onto the table. "Seven hundred dollars. The balance due on the viola. So we're even now, right?"

Lan stared longingly at the money. He could really use it to help his family, Sieu An and Johnny. But he couldn't touch it. Knowing where that money came from—and all the human suffering it had surely caused—filled him with revulsion.

"I can't take it," he said.

"What?"

"I can't take it. It's drug money. I tried to call you yesterday to tell you—I want to buy the viola back from you. It will be a while, you can keep it in the meantime, but I can't keep the money you've given me for it, and I can't take any more. I told you how I feel about it."

Adam looked at him hard. "Lan, this has nothing to do with you, where this money came from. Nothing at all. Nathaniel's got his financial situation worked out again, he gave me the money, and it's really none of your business where he got it."

"But he's a *drug dealer*," Lan insisted, keeping his voice low. "He's a criminal. He makes money off other people's misery." He studied Adam's big hands, turning the roll of bills over and over. "I saw your Jeep parked by my building last night. I think you or your brother were downstairs. And I think the people in

126

that apartment are the Trio you told me about. Who was in that apartment last night? Was it you? Or was it Nathaniel?"

"It was me," Adam said softly.

"You? What were you doing there, Adam? Are you in on the dealing, too?"

Adam sighed and rubbed his eyes. "I was taking a message to them from my brother. That's all. I offered to do it. I wasn't picking up drugs, I swear! Nathaniel's been in kind of bad shape lately, and I thought it was better for me to go than him. And I parked around the side of the building, because I figured you wouldn't notice the Jeep there. I guess I was wrong about that."

"Yes. You were wrong about that and . . . other things. Listen, Adam, I don't think I can help you any more with the viola practice. I don't think I can help you with anything. I'm sorry." He stood up and strode back to the kitchen, his hands shoved into his pockets to keep them from shaking.

Sunday, January 14

Angie and Jack sat on folding chairs arranged around the small stage at the Hispanic Heritage Center, clapping madly when Connie Montoya came out to take her curtain call. Angie's father sat at the end of the row with Connie's two little boys, who were applauding their mother and grinning at Angie.

"Oh, she's really good, isn't she, Jack?"

"She sure is. I could tell what was going on just by watching her. Your stepmother can really *act.*"

Everybody got up to go for refreshments, and people began clearing away the chairs to make room for dancing. In a moment Connie and the other actors had come out to join them, still in their stage makeup. Angie gave her stepmother a hug and introduced her and her father to Jack. She could read the question in Connie's bright eyes: *Is this a new boyfriend?* Angie shook her head almost imperceptibly, hoping Connie would catch her signal and Jack wouldn't. He was such a nice person; Angie didn't want to do anything to hurt him.

A long table was loaded with all kinds of traditional

food—guacamole, tamales, empanadas—and they helped themselves and wandered around the center, examining the displays of photographs: some historical of original Hispanic settlers, others more contemporary, such as those of young men with their low-rider cars. A mariachi band filled the hall with its bright, brassy sound. Angie couldn't help tapping her feet to the irresistible beat. Then Jack made a sweeping bow and said, "Señorita, would care to join me for whatever that is they're playing?"

"Oh, Jack! I'm not sure I know how to dance to that kind of music."

"Won't know until we try, will we?" He piloted her out onto the dance floor, where Connie and her father and a lot of older couples were dancing to the lively music. Even the little kids were making up their own steps. As Jack spun her around in his version of the dance, Angie remembered that Marcos wouldn't have been caught dead doing any of this. Marcos would have thought it was stupid, a waste of time; he would have wanted to go make out in Riverbend Park instead. Angie was now beginning to understand how much her life was changing since she had broken up with Marcos, expanding in all directions.

The apartment looked nice, Lan reassured himself. April had been right about those blue pillows on the sofa and the blue tablecloth. He had remembered to bring some leftover muffins from Red's and chocolate chip cookies for Johnny. He didn't think he had forgotten anything.

Lan had arranged with Red to be off for three hours this afternoon, and Red had told him he would be paid for those hours. "You do good work, Lan," the owner of the diner had said. "I'd like to reward you, let you know you're appreciated here."

Lan was grateful. Three hours' wages would cover the cab fare both ways.

He watched for the taxi from the front window. The parking lot was about half full, but the giant's panel truck was parked again in front of the downstairs apartment. There was no sign of the other two cars. And no Jeep. He had seriously considered calling the police, tipping them off about the Trio, but he had no real evidence, no actual proof. Only what Adam had told him.

Adam! Lan thought again of the scene at Red's yesterday. He didn't want to be cruel, but on the other hand, he simply did not want anything to do with drugs. There was no gray area here: if Adam was willingly in contact with men he knew were drug dealers, then there was nothing Lan could do about that. But he would have nothing further to do with Adam; the friendship was over.

April had intercepted Lan as he rushed into the kitchen after that last meeting. "What's wrong?" she had asked. "What happened out there? You still have a few more minutes on your break. Tell me, Lan!"

And he had told her about what he had seen the night before, about the money, his conversation with Adam, his decision.

"Lan, I can see why you don't want to take the money, even though I don't think I'd be that noble. But you shouldn't cut him off like that, just because he's being loyal to his brother."

Lan shook his head, not trusting himself to speak.

"Can't you cut him some slack? He needs you, Lan. You know what it is to need a friend! Don't desert him now."

"I have to get back to work," Lan said heavily. His mind was made up. But he couldn't help noticing that April was very cool to him after that.

When the taxi pulled in, Lan went down to meet them with money for the driver, but he found that Sieu An had already paid him. Johnny bounced out of the back seat, his arm still in a cast, waving and smiling. Sieu An followed, trying to restrain Johnny's exuberance. Lan led them up the stairs to his apartment.

"This is where you live now?" Johnny asked, his eyes wide with wonder.

"Yes," Lan said. "Do you like it?"

"Yeah!" Johnny raced toward the bedroom to investigate, while Lan and Sieu An followed more slowly. "Hey, Lan, this is neat! Ma, come and look!"

Lan was encouraged by Johnny's enthusiasm. Now if only Sieu An would react the same way. Of course he didn't really expect his sedate sister to go whooping through the apartment. Only five-year-old boys could get away with that. Lan smiled to himself and waited for Sieu An to say something.

"Very nice," she said at last, when she had gazed silently at the bedroom, the bathroom, the kitchenette, and they had returned to the living room.

"Thank you," Lan said in the same quiet tone. "I'm glad you like it. Shall I make some tea?"

"Please."

Lan turned on the flame under a kettle, one of April's Goodwill treasures. He had already arranged the muffins and cookies on a plate and set out three cups and three paper napkins. While he waited for the water to boil, he told Sieu An about the hotliners who had painted the walls and fixed the furniture and scrubbed the carpet. But he didn't tell her about the "friend" who had picked the blue pillows and the tablecloth and kettle. He wondered if Sieu An and April would like each other. Lan couldn't help contrasting his shy, reticent sister with his outgoing, outspoken girlfriend.

"Can I go outside and play?" Johnny asked.

Lan paused for a moment. Outside to play? He hadn't considered that before. There really wasn't any place to play—just a big parking lot. And was it safe down there? Surely the drug dealers wouldn't bother a little boy, but Lan was afraid to take the chance. "Better stay up here with us, Johnny," he said. He wished he had something for him to do. Then he remembered that Johnny liked to draw. Lan tore a sheet of paper out of his notebook and found a colored pencil. "Draw us a picture," he suggested.

"I can't," Johnny said. "I broke the arm I draw with."

"How did you break your arm, Johnny?"

Johnny shrugged. "It was a accident," he said. "I fell."

"Where did you fall?"

"In the alley, riding my bike." He picked up the pencil in his left hand and made some scribbles, to please Lan.

Lan glanced at Sieu An. Was that the truth? Sieu An smiled. "He will be more careful next time. But the cast is coming off soon."

Lan felt relieved. At least his worst fears were proved wrong. The water boiled, the tea was made. Lan poured them each a cup. He sat down at the table across from his sister and looked at her carefully. She appeared to be all right. Tired, maybe, but she always looked that way—maybe because she always *was* tired. And, except for his arm, Johnny looked fine, too.

They drank the tea, saying little. "Your job?" Sieu An asked. "Is it all right?"

"It's fine," Lan replied. He told her about Red paying him for the hours he was taking off this afternoon. "I was going to use that to pay for your taxi," he said.

"Not necessary," Sieu An said. "I have money for this."

Lan thought of Adam and the money he would have to pay back for the viola. He immediately shut the thought out of his mind. This was not the time to worry about that.

Lan poured them a second cup and decided not to wait any longer. Johnny had gone into the bedroom and set up Lan's chess set on the bed and was singing softly to himself.

"Sieu An," Lan began quietly. "This is my home, and now it is your home, too. I want you and Johnny to come and live here with me. There's plenty of room. You and Johnny would have the bedroom."

She shook her head slowly. "It's very nice," she said. "But you know that I can't do that. I have a husband. Husbands don't like it when their wives go to live with their brothers. Vietnam, America, it makes no difference. Wives stay with their husbands."

"For Johnny's sake," Lan pleaded. "I worry about him. And about you, too."

"Johnny is Wayne's son. Have you forgotten that? It is important for a son to be with his father. Just as it was important for you to be with our father when you were a boy."

"My father was good to me. He loved me. He gave his life for me!"

"And do you know for certain that Wayne does not love his son? That he is not good to him? That he

133

would not give his life for Johnny? You don't know any of these things, Lan. All you know for sure is that you do not get along with Wayne. The rest is not for you to know. It is between husband and wife."

Johnny came out of the bedroom carrying the black king and the white queen in his left hand and pretended to walk them across the end of the table. "There is something else," Sieu An said. "I would like you to come back to live with us."

"With you?" Lan was shocked; he had not expected anything like this.

"Yes. I have discussed it with my husband. He has said that he is sorry for what happened between you. He admits that he sometimes loses his temper. He has made me two promises. One, that he will learn to control his temper. Two, that we move to a larger apartment, so that you have your own room. I don't know about the first promise."

She allowed herself a small smile. "Americans say it is very hard to teach an old dog new tricks, and keeping his temper is a new trick for Wayne. But I know that the second promise is true, because we have already found a place, not far from the restaurant. That is one new trick I have taught him—he must not be stingy with money. Business is good. We have hired a helper in the kitchen. We are making a nice profit. That is why I can pay my own taxi fare to come to visit you." She smiled again. "I have at last convinced my husband that, as the Americans say, 'You can't take it with you.' Is that right?"

Lan nodded. He didn't trust himself to speak. Sieu An's words changed everything.

"And so you must come with us, Lan, where you belong. Not with strangers, even though they are

134

kind. Not living in this place. You belong with your family."

Lan was too stunned to say anything. Johnny came and hugged him with his good arm. "You gonna come with us, Lan?" he asked, gazing up at Lan with worshipful eyes.

Lan shook his head. "I don't know."

It was all completely unexpected. The disappointment and confusion Lan felt as he watched them leave was almost more than he could bear.

Tuesday, January 16

"The skiing is going to be wonderful this weekend," Nikki said from the back of Kurt's Alfa. "I hear they got about eighteen inches up in the mountains."

"Ummm."

Nikki leaned forward from the cramped space where she crouched behind the two bucket seats. "Do you like cross-country skiing, Michelle?" Nikki asked. "Or are you strictly into downhill?"

"Downhill," Michelle murmured, staring out the window.

"Downhill is exciting and fun," Nikki went on in a cheerful voice, "but I like the freedom of cross-country. No crowds, no expensive lift tickets, just a chance to be out in the snow."

"Ummm."

Kurt smiled to himself. Good old Nikki—she was doing her best to keep some kind of conversation going as they drove to the NA meeting, but Michelle was in no mood to talk. When he picked her up she had apologized: "I feel like such a total jerk," Michelle had said, her voice faltering, "that I don't even know what to say. I'm sorry, Kurt. Really sorry. I still can't believe I made such a scene in public with you."

"Forget it," he said. "It's over."

Since then she had said practically nothing. Now Kurt stopped by a run-down brick church. For a moment they stared at the dingy building. Other cars were arriving, and the three of them watched as a few people picked their way over the icy sidewalk toward the side door. Michelle inhaled harshly. "Look, I'm not sure I can go through with this," she said.

"Just remember we're here with you," Nikki said reassuringly.

"And if it gets to be too much, we split, right?" Kurt added. "You give the word when you think you've had enough."

"Okay. So let's go." Michelle opened her door and climbed out.

They took their places on scarred metal chairs in the church basement, bright lights glaring off shabby walls. At exactly seven o'clock, a heavyset man in overalls said, "My name's Walter. I'm an addict," and began the meeting with an explanation of what NA was all about.

Kurt counted more than twenty people of all ages. He stole a sidelong glance at Michelle, who sat with her elbows tight against her sides, staring at her leather purse on the table in front of her.

"My name's Grace," announced a large woman in a flowered blouse. "I'm an addict." Grace told a story of how an old boyfriend had come back to town and asked her to score some drugs.

Then it was Howard's turn, describing his "slip," his return to drugs, his struggle to get clean again. Next a skinny young woman not much older than Kurt described how she had always used drugs to escape un-

137

happiness, and how hard it was to stay off drugs and endure that pain.

Michelle, it seemed to Kurt, never took her eyes off her purse. Slowly the hour passed. Then everyone stood up and formed a circle, their arms around each other. Michelle broke for the door.

"I don't know," she said, gasping for air in the cold, still night outside the church. "I don't know if I can do it. There's so much *pain* in there."

"But they're facing it," Nikki said. "They're trying not to run away."

Kurt said nothing, but he kept his arm around Michelle's shoulders.

"I just don't know if I can do this," she kept saying. "I don't *know!*"

PART IV
Nathaniel

Wednesday, January 17

Lan was the first hotliner to arrive at Temporary 3-A after his afternoon exam. Jenny had insisted that they continue their hotline hours through exam week and have their regular meeting, and now Lan was glad that she had convinced them. Lan wanted to talk about Ninja.

One of the hotline's firm rules was that hotliners were not to get personally involved with their callers. A couple of months ago Kurt had gotten in a lot of trouble when he broke that rule, and everybody seemed to have learned something from his experience. But now Lan found himself in a similar situation. The difference was that Lan had had no idea in the beginning that Adam Wolf and Ninja were the same person. But he wasn't sure how to present Ninja's complicated story to the hotline without giving away Adam's identity.

Ms. Hawkins, their advisor, arrived moments after Lan. "How are the exams going, Lan?" she asked.

"Fine, so far," he said.

"I understand you have quite a hectic schedule these days. I don't see how you keep up with it."

"I'm not sure I *am* keeping up with everything, at least not the way I should," he confessed. Before he could say any more, or Ms. Hawkins could ask questions, the door burst open and a group of hotliners trooped in, talking and laughing, accompanied by Mr. Montgomery. Among them was April, who coolly turned away from him. They hadn't had lunch together all week because of their exam schedules, and Lan realized now that she had been avoiding him since Sunday.

"Before we get started," Ilana Feldman said, "I wanted to tell you that the gigantic anti-drug poster Jason put up on the main bulletin board last week with our signatures has attracted a whole lot *more* signatures. It really seems to be catching on. When this one gets filled up, we'll start another one."

"I added my name to it," Michelle announced suddenly. "After lunch today."

"You did?" Nikki asked incredulously. "That's wonderful!" She rushed over and threw her arms around Michelle. Kurt, grinning, joined them for a three-way hug. *Wonder what that's all about?* Lan thought to himself, watching them.

Mr. Montgomery nodded approvingly. "Good going, everybody. So what else is happening? Surviving your exams okay?"

Groans. "I was on duty yesterday," Jack Mertz reported. "I took five calls, and every single one of them was about exams and grades. History seemed to be the main terror-maker, with math running close second."

"Nothing on drugs?"

Jack shook his head. "No, and I was kind of hoping to hear from Ninja," he said. "That's one person I

142

think we ought to be able to help, and we haven't heard from him in several days."

Lan decided now was the time. "I want to tell all of you something," he said quietly, aware of the attention now focused on him. "I know who Ninja is. But I can't tell you anything about him." The room was warm, but Lan felt suddenly cold. "I want to make sure everybody understands. I don't think I'm breaking any rules. I didn't get involved with somebody who called—it's that somebody I was already involved with started calling. I guess I gave him the idea. And I can't tell you who it is, because that would be breaking a confidence. I wish I could, but I can't."

"It's all right, Lan," Steven Feldman announced. "I for one respect your professional judgment on this."

Lan looked hard at Steven. Was their 'shrink-in-training,' as Ilana and Jenny called him, being serious, or putting him on?

"Do you have any idea what Ninja's going to do about his brother?" Kristen asked.

"No. I don't think he knows yet." He wished he could tell them everything, about Adam, and their confrontation at Red's Diner on Saturday. He knew that Adam needed the hotline more than ever, now that Lan had made plain his hard line against all involvement with drugs. All he could do was hope that Adam-Ninja would call the hotline again.

And then, just before the meeting broke up, Rob made his announcement: "I have to tell you guys something," he began. "I'm leaving. My parents are going to Czechoslovakia for six months," he hurried on, "and I'm going with them."

There were murmurs of "Oh no!" and everyone glanced at Jenny, who had a brave smile fixed on her face. Rob went on to describe the photographic project

143

he'd be doing, and there were lots of questions from the hotliners with a mixture of excitement and disappointment. Jenny's smile didn't waver.

Lan was surprised when she came up to him afterward. "I brought the truck," she said, "so I can drive you to our place. Okay?"

"Thanks, Jenny." Only a few days ago Jenny had been on top of the world, excited about the article in the local paper she and Rob had done. Now she looked as though the bottom had dropped out of that world. And he couldn't blame her.

"Ninja really is Adam Wolf, isn't he?" Jenny asked as they drove to her house, Lan's bike in the bed of the truck. "He named himself after his motorcycle."

"It's an interesting coincidence," Lan murmured, looking out the window.

"Oh, come on, Lan! It's not an interesting coincidence, it's a *fact*."

Lan could be so stubborn, so close-mouthed, Jenny thought. Why wouldn't he just admit it? All these things going on, these secrets. Like Rob knowing all along that his parents were planning to go to Eastern Europe, or at least hoping to go, and he never said a word because he said he didn't want to upset her. It made her so mad, she wanted to *scream*.

Suddenly she burst out, "Oh, Lan, I don't really care about Adam or whether he's Ninja or if his brother is dealing or not. Rob's leaving, and that's the only thing I care about right now."

"I know," Lan said.

"Six months, Lan! Such a long time! I know it's a once-in-a-lifetime opportunity he'd be *crazy* to pass up, and I'm really excited for him, but—" She broke off abruptly.

144

"Oh, Jenny," Lan said gently. "It's good for him and bad for you. When does he go?"

"In a couple of weeks," she said miserably. "It's just not *fair*, Lan!"

"No," he agreed. "It's not. When did you find out?"

"Over the weekend. It's hard for him, too. He feels great about going and horrible about leaving. But you know what I keep thinking about, Lan?"

"Lissa," Lan said, after only a second's pause.

That was the amazing thing about Lan, Jenny thought. Most of the time you couldn't figure out what he was thinking, but he could almost always figure out what *you* were thinking. "Yes," Jenny said. "Lissa. Oh, Lan, is this why Lissa killed herself? Because she hurt so bad?"

"Jenny, it's not the same thing at all," Lan told her gently.

"I never knew how hard it must have been for her when Dave left. Lissa was the best. She was pretty and smart and talented and she *cared*. But she couldn't handle it when Dave left."

"Jenny, listen. Lissa didn't take her life because of Dave moving away," Lan said earnestly. "It may have been a factor, but it wasn't the only reason. Something else was really wrong to make her feel as bad as she did. You must know that, Jenny."

Jenny thought about it. Lan was right; she hurt a lot, all right, but not as badly as Lissa must have to do what she did. *I guess I'll never really understand why Lissa killed herself. None of us will. We'll only ever have little pieces of the puzzle, like Dave leaving. And our memories of Lissa and what a wonderful friend she was.* She sighed. "I know, Lan," she admitted. "You're right."

"One thing that you can do to help make it hurt less

145

is to talk to people about it, Jenny," Lan said "It's still going to hurt, but talking about it can make it easier to deal with it all."

She turned to him, eyes brimming. "Not right now," she said. "Later. I've got to drive this stupid truck."

"You want me to drive, Jenny? I've got my permit now. I've been practicing. I could get us there."

But Jenny clenched her hands tightly on the steering wheel. "Thanks, Lan," she said stubbornly. "But I'm not a total basket case *yet*."

Lan had never seen Jenny like this. It was plain that she really loved Rob, and this separation was going to be very hard for her. It made him think of April and how he'd feel if she'd moved away. Things were tense between them now; April was obviously upset about the way he was handling the situation with Adam. He didn't know how to deal with her anger.

His thoughts veered to Sieu An. So far he hadn't been able to tell anyone about her decision not to come and live with him. *Decision* wasn't really the right word; a decision meant a choice, and Sieu An seemed not even to have considered the idea. It was incredible—all the time he was making plans to get her to move in with him, she had been planning to have him move in with her and Wayne!

The snow that had been threatening all day began to fall while Lan was cooking. Fine, crystalline flakes quickly blanketed everything in a layer that gleamed like porcelain. "No way you're going to ride your bike home in this, Lan," Jenny said when they sat down to eat.

"And no way you're going to drive the truck in this, Miss Jenny," Mr. Haviland said. "You can stay here for the night, Lan, if you like. Your bed in the solar room is always available, you know. But if you'd rather go back to your apartment, I'll be happy to drive you."

Maybe it was selfish, Lan thought, but he really wanted to be in his own cozy place tonight. He wanted to study, to work on his kung fu, to be alone. "If it wouldn't be too much trouble . . ." he began, although he felt it probably was.

"Not at all," Mr. Haviland said. "But let's go now, before the storm gets any worse."

Jenny didn't protest, Lan noticed; nor did she offer to come along for the ride. Lan guessed she wanted to spend some time on the phone with Rob. She was probably counting every minute they had left.

Mr. Haviland eased the truck, with Lan's bike under a tarp in the back, out of the carport and onto the street. "Jenny tells me you're learning to drive," Mr. Haviland said as they slithered up to a red light.

"Yes." Lan was feeling worse and worse that he had asked Mr. Haviland to drive in such bad conditions. "A friend is teaching me." *Was teaching me*, Lan thought. *Now that's over, too.*

"Driving in this stuff is graduate level," Mr. Haviland observed, and they fell silent again.

It was an agonizingly slow trip, and Lan's neck ached with tension by the time they reached his neighborhood. His apartment complex was transformed by the thickening blanket of snow that covered the ugly brown dumpster and piled up on the edges of the concrete steps and the rusted iron railing of the balcony. The parked cars wore snowy caps, and only a few tracks marred the pristine whiteness of the parking lot. "Home Sweet Home," Mr. Haviland said as they uncovered the bike and lifted it down.

"Thank you," Lan said. "I'm really sorry you had to

147

come out on a night like this. Would you like a cup of tea before you go back?" he offered politely.

But Mr. Haviland declined his invitation, anxious to get home before the snow got any deeper. Frankly relieved, Lan climbed the stairs with his bike.

Later that night Lan heard an argument downstairs, voices rising and falling, an unmistakable tone of anger. Looking out between the slats of the blinds, Lan spotted the Jeep. It had only a thin accumulation of snow, so it hadn't been there long. Then a door slammed, and a tall, lanky figure dashed toward the Jeep. Not Adam, but someone who looked like him. Probably Nathaniel. The deep treads of the Jeep's tires bit into the snow as it drove away.

Lan checked his watch: nine o'clock. He had one exam scheduled for tomorrow, but as hard as it was snowing it was likely that school would be canceled. He sure hoped so; he didn't want to have to ride his bike to school in this stuff, beautiful as it was. He decided to give himself the night off from studying. One night, just to do what he felt like doing. Even if it wasn't canceled, he knew he was prepared.

Lan put on the loose-fitting pants and shirt that he wore to practice kung fu, made sure he had enough space to move freely without bumping into furniture, and began working through a *kata*, a sequence of movements, each named for the animal whose moves it mimicked: the mongoose . . . the white crane . . . the cobra. His mind was focused on the precision of each movement, his *chi* was really flowing. He felt powerful and in control. All sense of time vanished as he entered this inner world.

Someone was pounding on the door and shouting his name. Lan stopped, momentarily confused. He took off the chain lock and opened the door. It was

Adam, his motorcycle jacket and pants caked with snow.

"Have you seen the Jeep?" Adam gasped. "Has my brother been down there tonight?"

"I saw the Jeep earlier," Lan answered carefully. "It could have been Nathaniel."

"When?"

"About nine o'clock, I think. What time is it now?"

"After eleven. I've been waiting at his place. He said he had to go somewhere and then he'd be back. I figured he was coming here, to see those guys downstairs."

Lan wasn't sure what to do. He didn't really want to invite Adam in, but neither could he let him stand on his doorstep in the snow. "Would you like to come in?" he asked reluctantly.

Adam shook his head. "I've got to find him, Lan. I've got to make sure he's all right."

"He seemed all right when I saw him," Lan said. "He looked fine to me."

"You don't know him, Lan. You don't know what he's been like lately—depressed and paranoid. I'm really worried about him. He wouldn't tell me where he was going, but he said he'd be right back and to wait for him. But it kept getting later and later, and I got scared. I was afraid he came here to talk with them and . . . something happened."

"He looked fine to me," Lan repeated stiffly. He did not want to be involved in this; he thought he had made that plain the last time he had talked to Adam.

Now Adam gripped Lan's arm hard. "He's my brother, man! Don't you care about anything besides your stupid ideas about right and wrong? He's a human being! And he's in bad trouble!"

Lan tried to think how to react. April's words came

149

back to him: "He needs you, Lan. You know what it is to need a friend! Don't desert him now." But he was not ready to relent, to make friendship more important than principles.

"Is there any place else you think he could have gone?" he asked. "It's a bad night to be out driving. Maybe he decided to stay over with some friends, and in the morning you'll find out everything's all right." *You know what it is to need a friend*. Lan hesitated, wavering; maybe he should tell Adam not to go out in the snow, to stay here. But Adam was already turning around.

"Look, Lan, I'm sorry I bothered you. I guess your so-called crisis training doesn't count when you don't approve of what caused the crisis," Adam said bitterly. "I've got to go, I've got to find him."

Lan, barefoot and shivering in the cold doorway, watched Adam drive away, his rear wheel skidding dangerously as he turned onto the street.

Thursday, January 18

The sun rose in a brilliant blue sky. It had barely topped the mountains to the east when Lan picked his way over snowy sidewalks to the public telephone and called Jenny.

"Are we having school today?" he asked. "I'm sorry if I woke you, but I still don't have a radio."

"Don't worry, I'm up. It's a delayed opening—eleven o'clock. They say they'll have the streets clear by then, but I don't see how they can. Do you want me to come and pick you up, Lan?"

"No, thanks. I'll manage." His reply was automatic; Lan knew the roads would be tricky, but he still hated to accept favors. "I hope your father got home okay last night."

Assured that Jenny's father was fine, Lan dropped another quarter into the telephone and called Adam's house. It was still early, but he was sure Mrs. Wolf would be up.

"He stayed with Nathaniel last night, Lan," she said, without a trace of anxiety in her voice. Lan realized that she probably had no idea that Adam had

151

been running around the city in a blizzard looking for his brother. "I can give you the number, if you'd like to call him there."

Lan searched hastily for something to write with. "Could you give me Nathaniel's address, too, please?" he asked, jotting down the information.

"I imagine Adam will stay there today. We don't bother with delayed openings at Academy—we're either open or closed, and with as much snow as we got in this part of town there's not a chance of having school today. I'm going to put on a pot of coffee and spend a cozy day at home working on a quilt I'm making for Jed."

Trudging back to his apartment, his sneakers wet through, Lan thought how nice it must be to have a mother who made quilts and baked bread. He didn't like to admit it, even to himself, but he was worried about Adam. Where could he be? As he cut through the parking lot, he saw the door open to the apartment below his. The bald giant stepped outside, huge bare arms folded over his bare chest.

The giant nodded to Lan. "Snowed a lot," he said.

"Yes," Lan said, taking the steps two at a time.

By mid-morning the snow was melting, and dark patches showed in the parking lot. Lan checked the address Mrs. Wolf had given him: 327 Lehigh Street. That was in the university area, not far from the high school. Not too far out of his way. Maybe he could ride past Nathaniel's house and try to find out if Adam was there. Just because Lan was completely deadset against anything involving drugs didn't mean he wanted anything bad to happen to Adam. After all, they *had* been friends.

Lan carried his bicycle down the steps and set off carefully. The plows had cleared most of the main streets, which were now almost dry, but the side streets were still snowpacked and treacherous. Sometimes he simply gave up and walked his bike on the sidewalks. It was slow going.

Number 327 looked like any of the other small, adobe-style houses in that area, a couple of snow-laden bushes on a patch of white lawn. Nothing to distinguish it except the powerful black Kawasaki Ninja parked on the little porch. Apparently Adam had gotten back here safely last night—but there was no sign of the Jeep.

Lan hesitated. Should he go knock on the door? Adam might not mind, but Nathaniel was a different matter. Anyway, what did he have to say to Adam? Lan really hadn't changed his mind about anything. He kept on going, figuring he'd better stop worrying so much about Adam and concentrate on his physics exam.

Everything was in a state of confusion at the high school. The delayed opening had thrown the exam schedule off, and it was announced that tests scheduled for the morning would be made up next week; afternoon tests would begin right after lunch.

Lan went looking for April. He hadn't seen much of her this week. Monday had been Martin Luther King Day, a holiday, and their private lunch room was suddenly no longer available during exam week. He knew she was upset with him, and it bothered him that she wouldn't talk to him about it, give him a chance to make her see it his way.

He found her outside the cafeteria, talking with Kristen Hallett and Nikki Vavra. He didn't want to barge up to them and pull her away. He thought she saw him hovering around, but she seemed to be deeply involved in her conversation and ignored him. Lan walked away.

Exasperated and a little hurt, he went through the cafeteria line alone, carrying his tray to a relatively quiet corner to eat by himself. The cafeteria was always a noisy place, but he tried to ignore the chaos around him and concentrate on his sandwich. Out of the corner of his eye he watched April, Nikki, and Kristen go through the line and find seats near the big window facing the common with the tall flagpole in front of the school. Lan guessed that the snow was keeping a lot of students cafeteria-bound, away from the usual lunchtime hangouts. It did seem more crowded than usual, and he knew April would usually rather be caught dead than eating there.

Then Lan noticed that the noise level was escalating, and number of students were rushing toward the window. He heard someone shout, "Look! He's going to jump!"

Lan was on his feet in an instant. He saw April pushing her way toward him through the crowd. "Somebody's up on the tower," she said urgently when she reached his side. "I don't know who it is, but I think that's Adam Wolf out there by the flagpole."

He seized her hand. "Let's get out there and find out what's happening."

Most of the students were inside, crowding toward the window to watch the drama unfold, but some had begun pouring outside for a closer look. "Come this way," April said, pulling him after her. "I know the quickest way."

She led him through the library and out of the building by a back door Lan didn't even know existed. Running around the end of the building, Lan spotted

154

the Jeep parked haphazardly near the common. Quickly he took in the scene.

A tall, broad-shouldered figure was poised—feet together, arms flung wide—on the top of the brick tower that soared above the main entrance to the school. He looked as though he would at any moment spring off the tower into a graceful dive that could end only in disaster.

And crouched near the school flagpole was Adam Wolf. "Don't do it, Nathaniel! Please don't do it!" Lan heard Adam crying out, screaming at the figure balanced precariously far above him. People were racing out of the building toward Adam. Lan recognized a few of the teachers; Mr. Duckworth was among them.

"What's going on?" the vice principal shouted.

"My brother's up there! He's going to jump!"

"We'll get the police," Mr. Duckworth said. "Campus security will be here any minute." He ran heavily back toward the building.

"No cops!" Nathaniel screamed. "No cops, no cops, no cops!" he chanted. "One cop, and I jump. I swear it!"

Lan moved close to Adam and crouched beside him. Adam looked at him with panic in his eyes. "Let's try to keep him calm," Lan said softly. "What happened?"

"He's totally strung out," Adam said, his voice trembling. "He's been like this for a couple of days. We drove around all night. For hours, in the snow, after I found him. Then he wanted to come here. I thought it would help. He climbed up there somehow . . ."

"What the hell's going on down there?" Nathaniel shouted above Lan's head. "Who's that with you?"

"It's my friend, Lan," Adam shouted back.

"Nothing's going on. I just want you to come down, Nathaniel!"

"Oh, I'll be down, little brother! Wings outspread, flying flying—"

He was raving, Lan knew, not making sense. "He's going to kill himself," Adam said helplessly. "Oh God, Lan, I just don't know what to do. I talk and talk and nothing helps!" Adam's voice broke in a sob.

"It's not going to work to stand down here and yell at him," Lan said. "He needs to have somebody go up there and talk to him quietly. Calm him down."

Lan studied the situation. How had Nathaniel gotten up there, anyway? If Lan could figure a way to get up there too, he felt sure he could talk to him. Maybe Nathaniel would listen to him. It would be hard, because he was balanced so precariously. If Lan startled him, that would be it. And Lan would be responsible. But if he did nothing and Nathaniel jumped, Lan would feel responsible, too.

Lan spotted several of the hotliners in the growing crowd outside the building. Jenny, Rob, and Kurt were trying to get the gawkers to stay back, and Lan saw little Jason Aragon go toe-to-toe with a loud-mouthed student who began making crude jokes. Nikki and Kristen were hurrying toward Lan and April.

Lan stood up. "April," he said quietly, "you know this school building better than anybody. How can I get up there?"

"I know how to get you out on the roof," she said. "That's easy. But I don't know about the tower. I've never been there."

"Let's go then," Lan said. "This is his brother," he explained to Nikki and Kristen. "Stay with him, okay?"

Swiftly, April led him around to the back of the building. "The doors out onto the roof are usually

156

locked," she said. "But I know one that's easy to get open. I know for a fact that some of the teachers used to sneak out there to smoke, after they banned smoking on campus."

"How do you suppose he got up there?"

"I don't know. Maybe the same way. Nathaniel Wolf used to be a big deal here at Roosevelt. Former diving champion, all that. I remember hearing stories about him—I think he was into drugs even then. Maybe he hung out on the roof, too."

Lan raced after her up the stairs to the second floor, down the corridor, now nearly deserted as everyone flocked to witness the drama outside, and then up an odd little ramp to a closed door. "This is where they added the new wing," April told him. "I guess they decided not to break through here, or something, and they made the space into a staff lounge. So there's a kind of a dead space back there, and a spooky stairway with a little door at the top that leads out onto the roof. Now let's just hope I remember how to do this."

They hurried through the lounge and slipped into a tiny kitchen area. April opened a door to what appeared to be a storage closet and showed Lan a stairway leading up. "That's it," April whispered. "Be careful, Lan. Good luck."

Lan made his way up the stairs in the darkness and felt for the doorknob. Carefully he pushed the door open a crack and peered out into brilliant sunlight. He couldn't see much except the solid brick tower straight ahead of him, but he could hear Nathaniel shouting and people down below shouting back.

Lan stood motionless, trying to think what to do. He could, he decided, try to get out of the door and across the roof to the base of the tower before Nathaniel noticed him. Then he would figure out how Nathaniel had gotten to the top.

But before Lan could make his move, Nathaniel seemed to sense that someone was there with him.

"Who's there?" he demanded, not loud. Lan kept still by the barely open door. "I know somebody's up here," he said. "and I want to know who it is." Lan heard the edge of hysteria in Nathaniel's voice. He had to do something *now*.

"It's Lan," he said simply, pushing open the door a little more. He could see Nathaniel now, poised on the top of the tower. "A friend of Adam's."

"The guy with the viola?"

"Yes."

Nathaniel laughed insanely. "What do you want, pal?"

Lan didn't move a muscle, careful to keep his voice calm and quiet. "I came to talk to you."

"Nothing to talk about." Suddenly Nathaniel's attention shifted to the crowd below him. "No cops, no cops, no cops," he began to chant again.

"The cops won't bother you," Lan said. "I promise." He hoped it was true. "Would you come down here and talk?"

But Nathaniel's voice hardened. "I can talk from here. What do you want to talk about?"

Lan made one step toward the tower, but Nathaniel screamed at him, "Stop!" and Lan stopped.

"I want to talk about why you want to jump off this building," Lan said. "About why you want to kill yourself. Talk to me, Nathaniel. Please."

Later, Lan had no idea how long he waited on that cold rooftop, trying to keep Nathaniel talking. Most of what Nathaniel said didn't make sense to Lan. He didn't seem to be able to complete a thought before he

158

would veer wildly in some other direction, always blaming the Trio, his parents, his diving coach, *somebody*, for all the things that had gone wrong in his life. Lan didn't argue. Mostly he listened.

"Don't you want to come down?" Lan coaxed. "It must be cold up there. And you must be tired."

"Yeah, it is," Nathaniel admitted. "I am."

In another few minutes, Lan thought, he might have talked him down safely, but at that moment the police rescue vehicles arrived, sirens wailing, lights flashing. Nathaniel freaked. But instead of swandiving from the top of the tower, he jumped down onto the roof and made a frenzied rush at Lan. "You bastard!" he screamed, lunging for Lan.

Lan was ready for him. The harmonious movements of the kung fu *kata* were weapons when you needed them, and in a moment Lan had subdued Nathaniel. When the police finally made their way up onto the roof, they found Lan cradling Nathaniel in his arms like a child, while Nathaniel wept.

Wednesday, January 31

Jenny scanned the people who had gathered in Temporary 3-A. Everybody was there—everybody except Rob.

Rob had left three days ago, flying to New York on a Sunday morning with his parents. She would never forget their last night together.

She had wanted it to be a perfect evening, a perfect memory to carry with her in the lonely months ahead. She had spent a long time deciding what to wear, so that Rob would remember her looking really *nice*. Rob had made reservations at a great restaurant, and the meal looked delicious, but somehow she couldn't swallow. The lump in her throat kept getting in the way, and tears were constantly threatening to fill her eyes and run down her cheeks. She felt like such a *jerk* when she couldn't keep from crying.

Then Rob had suggested they go for a drive and headed for Riverbend Park. He parked the purple Volkswagen, reached for Jenny, and pulled her close. "I'll miss you," he said. "But the time will go by fast.

You'll see. And then I'll be back. We'll see each other before I leave for college."

He kissed her eyelids, her nose. "Anybody at your house tonight?" he asked.

"No," she breathed. "They went out somewhere and won't be back until late."

"Then let's go there. So we don't freeze to death."

Rob had built a fire in the fireplace. Kiss after hungry kiss, they drew closer until they were lying in each other's arms on the sofa in the glow of the firelight.

"Jenny—" Rob began, brushing her cheek with his fingertips.

Jenny knew what he was going to say, and her head was spinning crazily. She fought for control. "The thing is, Rob, I want it to be *right,* you know what I mean? Not when we're in a big hurry, or miserable because you're going."

"I understand, Jenny."

Because there didn't seem to be any more to say, they ended up watching television until her parents came home. Rob shook hands with both of them, they wished him luck, and Jenny walked numbly with him to the door. "Good-bye, Jenny," he whispered, kissed her lightly on the lips, and was gone.

Sunday she had moved through the day in a kind of trance, although her parents had tried to distract her, taking her out for supper to a place they liked, the Saigon Café, even though Lan no longer worked there. When they got home around eight, there was a message on the answering machine. It was Rob, calling from the New York Airport between planes. "I just want you to know, Jennifer Haviland," said the scratchy voice on the tape, "that you are the most important thing in my life. And I will not forget you, not

161

for one minute during the next six months, or however long it is. Believe it, Jenny. Love you. Bye."

She was desolate that she had missed his call, but she played the message over and over.

"I just wanted to tell you all," Jenny said when there was a break in the hotline discussion, "that Rob and I have another feature article coming out in the *Tribune*. This one's about the hotline. I got a call from the editor telling me it's been accepted."

"Congratulations, Jenny!" Mr. Montgomery said while the other applauded. "That's wonderful. You're our regular Lois Lane."

Lois Lane. That's what Rob used to call her. Jenny swallowed the lump of tears that was swelling in her throat and managed a brave smile.

Poor Jenny! Angie thought. She knew how awful her friend must be feeling, and she knew, too, there wasn't much anybody could do. Angie remembered when she was first breaking up with Marcos, how bad she felt all the time, almost believing that she would be miserable for the rest of her life. You don't realize that after a while it stops hurting, Angie was thinking, and then things start getting better again.

Now everything seemed to be getting better for Angie. She had gone back to the Hispanic Heritage Center after the fiesta and applied for a job. There weren't any openings, but the director said she could do volunteer work for a while, and something might come up.

"I'll be at the main desk on Sunday afternoons, handing out brochures and answering questions, maybe in Spanish," she had told Jack. "And you know what else? I'm thinking about going to the community college after I graduate and taking courses in Southwest history, Chicano studies, things like that."

162

"Fabuloso," Jack had said.

Jenny needs somebody like Jack, Angie thought; a really good friend.

Kurt saw the hurt in Jenny's eyes and wished he could help her. He knew how much she must be missing Rob. Maybe he could invite her to Popeye's just to talk. Not that long ago, Kurt reflected, it wouldn't have occurred to him to ask someone out just to be a friend. Asking someone out would have meant a date.

A lot had changed since Kurt had been involved with the hotline, and the changes were important to Kurt. He hoped he was a better person because of it; he knew he was a better friend. He flashed on his sister Dana. Yeah, he was a better brother, too.

Kurt's eyes flicked over the group and rested on Michelle. She was looking a little better lately, since Nikki had taken her under her wing. Michelle still had a long way to go, according to Nikki, but she had good friends who'd help her get there. Kurt was glad he was one.

Kurt thought again about Jenny. This was a bad time for her, even though she was putting up a brave front. *I hope things work out for you too, Jenny. You deserve it.*

"Lan?"

His head snapped up. Everybody seemed to be looking at him. Had he missed something? "Yes? I'm sorry, my mind was somewhere else."

Ms. Hawkins smiled at him warmly. "We're wondering how it's going for you, Lan. This seems to be a time of change for several people in the hotline. Sometimes it's a good idea to let the callers go for an hour or two and see how the *listeners* are doing."

163

"I'm doing fine," he said, but Ms. Hawkins didn't take her eyes off him.

"You want to tell us what you're doing?"

This was always hard for him. Lan wasn't used to dumping his problems in front of other people, but when he looked around the room, at the concerned expressions on every face, it struck him again that these really were his friends.

"Well, I moved in with my sister and her family," he began slowly. "They got a bigger apartment, so now I have my own room. I'm keeping my job at Red's, though, because it's better if I don't work with my sister's husband."

He had been nervous about that first meeting with Wayne, but his brother-in-law was on his best behavior. The big, red-faced man had actually apologized to Lan, told him he was sorry for the way he had behaved and what he had said, and he promised to try to do better. Lan had grasped the hand Wayne extended to him and shaken it. "I'm glad to be back with my family," he had said stiffly. And then he had told Wayne and Sieu An that he would keep on working at Red's but that he would pay his share of the rent and food. They had accepted that.

Then he had worked out that remarkable deal with Rob for the VW. It was Rob's idea. "It's got a lot of miles on it, but it's in terrific shape," Rob had said. "You can rent it for as long as I'm gone, fifteen dollars a month. Its better than having it sit in a garage for six months."

The offer had come at exactly the right time. It would be cheaper to live with his sister's family, and once he got the rent and utility deposits back on the apartment, he would be able to pay off most of what he owed on the viola. The viola that had been Lissa's and then became Adam's. Now it would be his again.

"And what about Ninja?" Mr. Montgomery asked. "Any news on Adam and Nathaniel?"

Lan felt April's hand gently cover his hand, her fingers laced with his. Sometimes it made him uncomfortable when she was so open about her feelings for him, but now he was glad to have her there.

"Nathaniel's in a treatment center. Adam seems to be doing better, now that his brother is safe. He barely made it through the reauditions of the Youth Symphony on Saturday, but he did make it."

"Lan deserves most of the credit for that," April said. "He spent a lot of time tutoring Adam. I don't know if you all know that or not."

"Lan deserves a lot of credit for a lot of things!" Jenny said. "I still can't get over how you went up on the roof and actually managed to get Nathaniel down off that tower. That is just about the most dramatic thing I've ever heard of."

Lan squirmed. He had become something of a hero at Roosevelt High, and he was extremely uncomfortable with the attention.

"There's more," April said. "Did you tell them about the police raid?"

There was a general clamor. "Police raid? Come on, Lan! Tell us about it!"

"The police raided the apartment below mine," he explained. "They set up a listening post in my bathroom, and they were able to arrest the Trio, the drug organization Nathaniel worked for. I didn't have anything to do with that," he added.

"It sounds pretty scary, though, Lan," Ms. Hawkins commented.

"It was," he admitted. "That was a part of my decision to move in with my sister and her family again. I decided I didn't want to live there anymore. It wasn't worth it." *I'd still rather be on my own. But the time isn't right yet.*

April's hand tightened over his. He recalled the conversation they had had right after the rooftop scene. "What I want to know is, what made you change your mind, Lan?" she had challenged him. "I thought you wouldn't help people who were involved with drugs, no matter what."

"I was wrong," he had admitted to her. "When I'm a doctor, I won't decide who deserves help and who doesn't. I'll help whoever needs it. Adam needed it, and so did Nathaniel. I just did what I had to."

Now he smiled at her, and she smiled back.

What to Do If You Need Help

Although the book you have just read is fiction, these situations are real and can happen to anyone. If you or someone you care about has a problem there are numerous services you can ring for help. Listed below are the names and telephone numbers of some of the organisations available which can offer information, counselling and a sympathetic ear to young people in need.

THE SAMARITANS

24 hours a day, 365 days a year
The Samaritans are available at any time to anyone who needs someone to talk to.

If you are feeling desperate and alone — you may even have come to the point when you feel life is no longer worth living — they may be able to offer you support. Every year nearly 4,500 people kill themselves and over 200,000 people attempt suicide. Nearly 600 people under 25 take their own lives each year. Many of these don't want to die: they just don't want to go on living as things are.

The Samaritans are there when things are too much for you. They'll listen to how you feel, whatever the reason is. Samaritans volunteers are of all ages from 18 up, and from all walks of life. They are ordinary people who are good listeners and who care about people. They won't tell you what to do, or be shocked by anything you say. They aren't religious and they don't make judgements. Most importantly, they won't tell anyone about you or your call unless that's what you want. You don't even have to tell them your name.

There are 185 Samaritan branches throughout the UK.

You'll find the address and telephone number of your nearest branch in the telephone book or from directory enquiries. You can ring them 24 hours a day, every day of the year. You can visit the branch in the day time and evening and you can write to them too.

CHILDLINE

Freephone 0800 1111, 24 hours a day, 365 days a year
Childline is a free, national helpline for young poeple in trouble or danger. It provides a confidential telephone counselling service for any child or young person with any problem at any time. Trained counsellors provide support and advice and can refer young people in danger to appropriate helping agencies.

SHELTER NIGHTLINE

Freephone 0800 446441, 6 pm to 9 am Monday to Friday, 24 hours a day Saturday and Sunday, 365 days a year
Shelter provides this free, national helpline to give advice and assistance to people in need of housing. If you need help between 9 am and 6 pm on a weekday (when the Nightline is closed), ring Shelter's head office number, 071 253 0202.

MESSAGE HOME

071 799 7662, 24 hours a day, 365 days a year
This number connects young people who have run away from home with a telephone answering machine on which you can leave a message to be passed back to your family. You don't have to give any details, except the name and address of the person to whom you are sending your message; it will be passed on, in confidence, as soon as possible.

NATIONAL AIDS HELPLINE

Freephone 0800 567123, 24 hours a day, 365 days a year
This free, national helpline is staffed by trained counsellors at all times; their aim is to provide advice, information and emotional support on HIV, AIDS and drug-related matters.

They have three additional freephone numbers offering the same service in other languages at specified times:

Freephone 0800 282445 – Bengali, Hindi, Gujarati, Punjabi and Urdu, 6 pm to 10 pm Wednesday

Freephone 0800 282446 – Cantonese, 6 pm to 10 pm Tuesday

Freephone 0800 282447 – Arabic, 6 pm to 10 pm Wednesday

BROOK COMPUTERISED HELPLINE

071 410 0420, 24 hours a day, 365 days a year
This computerised helpline gives recorded advice on contraception, pregnancy and related matters, and information on where to go for further information. The telephone number of your nearest Brook Advisory Clinic can be found in the telephone book or from directory enquiries, or ring the Brook Advisory Central Office on 071 708 1234 between 9 am and 5 pm Monday to Thursday, 9 am to 4.30 pm Friday.

FAMILY PLANNING ASSOCIATION

071 636 7866, 9 am to 5 pm Monday to Thursday, 9 am to 4.30 pm Friday
Family Planning Clinics offer advice and help with contraception, pregnancy and related matters. The telephone number of your nearest clinic can be found in the telephone book or from directory enquiries, or ring the Family Planning Association Central Office at the number given above.

TURNING POINT

071 702 2300, 9.30 am to 5 pm Monday to Friday
Turning Point runs over 40 projects throughout the UK offering help to people with drink, drug and mental health problems, and to their friends and relations. If you or a member of your family has a problem of this kind, their Central Office is contactable at the number given above and can offer you counselling or refer you to your nearest relevant organisation.

RAPE CRISIS CENTRE

071 837 1600, 10 am to 11 pm Monday to Friday, 9 am to midnight Saturday and Sunday
This number connects you to the London branch of the Rape Crisis Centre, which offers confidential counselling by women to women and girls about sexual violence. It doesn't have to be an emergency for you to call them and if necessary you can reverse the charges. They can also refer you to your local Rape Crisis Centre for counselling over the phone or face-to-face.